EYE OF DANGER

TIGER'S EYE MYSTERIES

ALYSSA DAY

HOLLIDAY PUBLISHING, LLC

1

L ife tip 101: When anybody says to you: "We need to talk" ...
     Run for the hills.
Fast.
(Unless you're already in the hills. Then run for the valleys. Or the beach. Just ... run.)

~

W e were at the opening of the newly dedicated Dr. Linda Parrish and John Luke Arnold Museum of Pirate History when my uncle pulled me aside and said four terrifying words:

"We need to talk."

"Nothing good ever started with those four words," I said, my spirits plummeting. "Who died?"

"Nobody died," Uncle Mike said, his face shadowed. "It's your father."

My father had abandoned me— abandoned all of us— when my mother died.

"What about him?"

"He's on his way back to town, and he says he's in trouble."

Jack—my friendly neighborhood private investigator, and maybe something more—tightened his hand around mine. "We'll handle it together. After witches, leprechauns, gators, and the Fae, how bad could it be?"

I'd heard some of those gators had never been caught. Still ...

"You know what you should never, ever say? *'How bad could it be?'*"

Here we go again.

"I need donuts."

~

"Is there anything better than a sunny morning at Dead End's best pawnshop?" Eleanor practically sang out the words when I walked into work the next morning, worries about my long-lost father still hamster-wheeling around my brain.

I raised an eyebrow. "Last I knew, we were Dead End's only pawnshop. Or is there something you want to tell me?"

She shrugged. "Only. Best. Most awesome. All are true. And guess who brought in seven new items in pawn and rang up almost $500 in sales so far today?"

"Nice! You are my favorite employee." I grinned at her while I walked over to put my bag in the drawer behind the counter. "*Definitely* my favorite employee."

"I'm your only employee."

"Only. Best. Most awesome. All true."

She laughed and went back to filling out paperwork on the new intakes, and I took a moment to look around at what truly was the most awesome pawnshop in the world, at least in my somewhat biased opinion. Sparkling clean and neatly arranged, from the aisle of electronics to the magical potions counter, I loved every inch of it, even the walls, now that I'd finally sold the dreamcatcher that had an authentic nightmare trapped in its woven threads. It was a good business, and I got to meet interesting people and occasionally discover interesting artifacts, and it was even modestly profitable.

And it was all mine.

I'd never wanted to be a doctor, or a lawyer, or a captain of industry. For a brief time, before the onset of my unique ability changed my life, I'd thought about studying art history. Maybe traveling the world to study ancient artwork in some kind of artist-meets-Indiana Jones job that probably only existed in my imagination. Instead, I'd become the manager, and then owner, of my very own pawnshop, in the same town where I'd been born and lived my entire life.

And, I had to admit, I loved every minute of it. Well, except for the two times people had dumped dead bodies on my back porch, but I had to hope that would never happen again.

"Seven items, huh? Does that include this? Again?" I eyed the stuffed Jackalope on the counter—a jackrabbit with antelope horns attached, taxidermied to look as if the creature had actually existed—and could feel my lips curl back. It wasn't even cute, and I had no idea why anybody would want to keep making the things.

Then I blinked. Given the world we lived in today, with vampires and shifters and witches and Fae all walking around, right out of the pages of fairytales and into our neighborhoods and towns, maybe Jackalopes *did* exist.

I took a closer look.

Maybe?

Nah. That had to be glue around the base of the horns. Anyway, we had to draw the line somewhere. I glanced up and noticed that Eleanor was pointedly not meeting my gaze.

"I see Mr. Oliver was in again. How many times is he going to pawn this guy? Also, and not that I don't appreciate the business, but the man has a very successful plumbing company. Why does he need that fifty bucks so much every month? Does he have a deep, dark, gambling problem that nobody knows about?"

Eleanor's pale cheeks—"a Southern lady always wears a hat to protect her skin, Tess"—turned pink, clashing with the pristine red Dead End Pawn polo shirt she wore with white capri pants and red sandals. "I'm sure that Bill, I mean, Mr. Oliver, has no such thing. He just, ah, I think, um, he ..."

The light finally dawned in my apparently clueless brain. "He keeps coming in here to see *you*, doesn't he?"

"I don't know what you're talking about, Tess." She grabbed the paperwork and clutched it to her chest. "I'm going in the back and finishing this up, away from any *distractions.*"

I started laughing. "I'd think *Bill* would be more of a distraction than I am. Good for you, you man magnet, you."

She shot me a *Look*, but her cheeks, flaming red by now, told me I'd been right. I just grinned but didn't tease her anymore. She was in her early sixties, and she'd been alone for a long time since her husband died. If she found romance with Mr. Oliver, who was a very nice man, then good for her. I was still smiling when I put the Jackalope back up on the shelf next to Fluffy, the ancient taxidermied alligator who served as our shop mascot.

Thinking of romance made me think of other things,

though, like *dates*, which made me think of a certain hot tiger shifter whose detective agency's office shared the building with my pawnshop. As if my thoughts had called to him, the connecting door he'd requested be built between our two establishments opened, and six feet, four inches of bronze-haired, hard-muscled deliciousness sauntered in, his summer-grass-green eyes sparkling in his gorgeous, tanned face.

"Eleanor has a suitor?" Jack grinned at me. "I can almost feel sorry for the man. She'll have him wrapped around her finger just like she does with the customers who come in here. And if he gets out of line, she can always shoot him."

"Hey! That was *one* time!"

Eleanor was my secret weapon. She loved people and adored bargaining and negotiated great deals that made everyone happy. Repeat business is the heart and soul of a pawnshop's business, especially in a small town, and she was a great part of our team.

I rolled my eyes. "Just because you have *superior tiger hearing*, that doesn't mean you need to weigh in on every conversation you eavesdrop on."

"Hey, I came over to invite you to lunch. The eavesdropping was just a bonus."

I glanced across at the antique cherrywood grandfather clock. "It's ten a.m."

"Breakfast?"

"You told me you ate a dozen donuts on the way to the opening!"

"Exactly." He patted his unfairly flat abdomen. "I'm wasting away."

"Maybe later. Like at noon. Eleanor has granola bars in the back, if you're dying."

He grimaced. "I'd rather eat tree bark."

I threw up my hands. "Then turn into a kitty and go catch some furry snacks. I have a business to run here."

The man who turned into a quarter-ton Bengal tiger raised an eyebrow. "A *kitty*?"

He glanced pointedly around my empty shop. "And, yes. I can see how you're swamped."

"Don't you have crimes to solve? More lost pets to find?"

"Are you going to add the Jackalope to your mascot shelf with Fluffy?"

I pinned him with my most commanding stare, and he blinked.

"Tess, are you in pain?"

"No. Argh. That was my commanding—never mind. Tell me, shifter boy, are Jackalopes real?"

"Shifter boy?" His eyes lit up with wicked glee. "I'll be happy to demonstrate that I'm actually shifter *man*, if you like."

"Right here?" I may have squeaked out the words, but I was proud that I didn't retreat when he took a step toward me. "No! I mean, whatever, just tell me about Jackalopes."

He laughed but then shrugged. "Your guess is as good as mine. I rode through a place out west once that had a giant statue of one in the middle of town. So, maybe?"

I frowned at it. "I think I'll continue to believe that they're not, because it would be awful if they're a rare species, and the only known example is dead, stuffed, and playing matchmaking go-between in my pawnshop."

Jack made a face. "Just promise me that you'll never take any stuffed tigers. That would run a little too close to home."

"I can definitely promise you that." My heart gave a painful twinge at the idea of an animal as magnificent as a tiger stuffed and on display in a shop. "And this conversation just took a dark turn. Go away. I have work to do, counters to polish, money to count, world domination to plan. Go investigate something."

"I might investigate if Mellie has anymore donuts."

My stomach said *yes, yes,* but my jeans' tight waistband said *no, no.* I settled for moderation. "Save me one. Um, maybe two. But not the cream-filled."

See? I can be reasonable. Practically a deprivation diet.

He leaned on the counter and flashed a slow, sexy, smile at me. "My calendar is clear. So after I get donuts, I think I'll spend the day planning our date. Which day did you decide on?"

Busted.

I swallowed, hard, and grabbed for my phone, opening the calendar app and pretending to study it to buy myself time. "Um."

"Tess." He sighed and gently took the phone out of my hands, his smile fading. "You've obviously changed your mind, and that's okay. I'd never pressure you. Let's just forget about it."

The flash of hurt in his eyes was there and gone so fast that I almost didn't see it.

Could have lied to myself that I *didn't* see it.

I try really hard not to lie to myself, though.

"Tess?"

"This Saturday," I blurted out. "Let's do it this Saturday."

His grin made me realize what I'd said, and I could feel the heat rush up my face. "Do it as in go out. On the date. Not *do* it, do it. I mean—"

He put his hand on mine. "I get it. No *doing it* involved or expected. Just a simple date."

I blew out a breath. "Nothing with you is ever simple. Now go away, so I can get to work."

Before he could answer, the door to the back room

smashed open, and Eleanor staggered out, her face drained of all color, holding her phone out toward us. "Dave. *Dave.* Help me! Jack ..."

Jack took one look at her and snapped into action, leaping toward her and catching her in one strong arm as she collapsed, taking the phone out of her hand and putting it to his ear. "Jack Shepherd here. What's happening?"

As he listened, an expressionless mask snapped down onto his face, reminding me that this same man who teased me and joked with me had spent ten years as a rebel leader and soldier, fighting in the most dangerous situations possible.

"Understood," he said. "On our way." He ended the call and speared me with a look. "We need to take Eleanor to the hospital. Can you close the shop?"

I grabbed my purse. "Of course. What is it? What's wrong?"

Eleanor's eyes popped open, and she cried out; a terrible, hoarse sound I never wanted to hear again. "It's Dave. My son. Dave's been shot."

2

J ack made the thirty-mile drive in less than twenty minutes, which would have terrified me if I hadn't been so busy comforting Eleanor and telling her over and over again that Dave was going to be just fine. The hospital was on the outskirts of Orlando, which is why the drive was so far. Dead End, population five thousand on a good day, was way too small for us to have our own hospital or even a good urgent-care clinic. For years, the only doctor we had also served as the county coroner, and he was a grouchy old man with the personality of a constipated gargoyle, so nobody went to him unless they were desperate.

"He's in surgery," I reported, one hand holding Eleanor's and the other holding my phone. "I've got Julio Martinez on the line, and he says they took him into surgery."

Eleanor clenched her jaw shut so tightly I could hear her teeth grinding. Then she took a deep breath and did what Southern women had been doing for hundreds of years— she stiffened her spine and shoved her fear and pain down deep, so she could take care of business.

"Right. Tell him we'll be there in two minutes," she said, and Jack took the corner into the parking lot so fast it was a wonder his old truck didn't tip over.

We parked and ran up to the surgical waiting area to find that it was chaos. The room was all white walls and orange plastic chairs, and it smelled of antiseptic and sweaty construction workers. Julio, Dave's right-hand man, and what looked like all the rest of Dave's employees, both the full-time people and the seasonal hires, crowded around the vending machine, wearing *Wolf Construction* shirts, jeans, work boots, and concerned expressions. They'd clearly walked off job sites to rush over to stand vigil for their boss, and August in Florida was what hell would be like if you added miserable humidity. So, it was a sweaty, dirty group, which didn't stop Eleanor for even a second from rushing over and straight into Julio's arms for a big hug.

She wasn't just the boss's mom, after all. She knew all of these men and women. Knew their kids' names. Had baked them birthday cakes, wrapped holiday gifts, and taught them at Sunday School. She was one of the best people I knew, and everybody loved her.

"She'll have plenty of support to get through this," Jack said, putting an arm around me. "Starting with you, me, and your family. It's going to be okay, Tess."

I took a deep, shaky breath and only then realized that I was trembling. I'd known Dave since I was a little girl, and he was a good friend. I leaned against Jack's shoulder and then yanked my head back when I felt it vibrating.

"Jack," I hissed. "You're growling."

The lines of his face looked as if they'd been carved in granite, and his eyes glowed with hot amber flames. Dave had been one of *Jack's* best friends since he was a kid, too.

Whoever had hurt Dave was going to be very, very sorry.

The doors that led to the operating rooms whooshed open, and a tall woman with warm brown skin, who looked to be around my age and wore surgical scrubs, walked out and looked around. "Dave Wolf's family?"

Eleanor looked at me, and I rushed over to her and took her hand in mine again. "We're his family," I told the doctor, when Eleanor didn't seem able to speak. "This is his mother, Eleanor Wolf."

The doctor, compassion in her dark brown eyes, held out her hand to shake Eleanor's. "Mrs. Wolf, I'm Dr. Boston. First, let me reassure you. Dave is doing just fine."

Eleanor's closed her eyes for a moment. "Praise God. Thank you so much, Doctor. What ... what can you tell me?"

She smiled. "Well, first off, if you're going to get shot, he picked a pretty good spot to get shot in."

Julio started laughing. He stuffed a fist in his mouth to try to stifle it, but such an expression of sheer relief lit up his face that I couldn't even be annoyed with him.

"What do you mean?" Jack demanded. I hadn't realized he was standing so close behind me until he spoke. "Where did he get shot?"

"In the side of the ass, in technical medical terms," the doctor said, one side of her mouth quirking up. "He said he turned and threw himself out the window, headfirst, when the man pulled the gun. The butt shot is the first piece of luck. The fact that the window was open at the time is the second."

"He always was one to turn the other *cheek*," Jack murmured from behind me, and I had to bite my lip against the bubble of hysterical laughter that threatened to burst out of my mouth.

Dr. Boston cast an amused glance at Jack, but then she turned serious. "The biggest piece of luck, I'm told, is that

Mr. Martinez was pulling into the parking lot when it happened, and he pulled Dave into his truck and got out of there before anymore shooting occurred."

"Who did this?" Jack demanded, but she shook her head.

"That's not my department. The sheriff is on her way, I understand. The bullet will still be at the scene, since it went all the way through Mr. Wolf's ... ah ... posterior. We cleaned the wounds and sutured, and he should be good to go soon, but I'd like to keep him overnight just to be safe, since you don't live within a ten-minute drive of the hospital."

She smiled at Eleanor, who was still clutching her hand. "Mrs. Wolf, if you'll come with me, you can see Dave now." She glanced around at the crowd hanging on her every word. "The rest of you can see him soon, but only two at a time. We don't want to overwhelm the other patients."

"Tell him we'll be right *behind* his mom," Jack murmured, and I threw him an elbow, which was like ramming my elbow into an iron door.

Ouch.

Julio finally let the laughter out, relief shining brightly in his eyes. "Yeah, and tell him we'll be sure to get to the *bottom* of this."

Dr. Boston rolled her eyes, but I could tell she was trying not to smile. She took Eleanor back to see Dave, and I blew out the breath I'd been holding. When I glanced back at Jack, any trace of humor on his face had vanished, and his eyes were flashing amber fire again.

"Jack?"

"I didn't want to alarm Eleanor, Tess, but just because Dave got lucky doesn't mean this isn't serious." He took my hand and pulled me away from the crowd, over toward the window. "Someone shot my friend. Someone is going to pay for that."

"Dave could have been killed," I said, the full impact hitting me now that I wasn't in comforting mode. "Jack, why would someone shoot Dave? Everybody loves Dave!"

My hands started shaking with reaction, and Jack pulled me in for a hug. I rested my forehead on his chest for a moment, trying to think clearly, trying not to waste time wondering why anybody would shoot Dave, because I had no idea, and instead thinking of what I should do next.

"I need to call Aunt Ruby and Uncle Mike. They'll want to come out and be here for Eleanor." I dug for my phone and called Uncle Mike's phone, because he'd be easier to explain this to, not that I knew much, yet. A minute or two later, I'd filled him in, and he'd promised he and Aunt Ruby would be out as soon as he fed the animals.

The doors opened again, and this time a short, blonde, pretty nurse came out and beckoned to Jack. "Mr. Wolf would like to see you now," she said, giving him an admiring glance. "If you'll follow me?"

He looked at me, and I nodded, and I even managed not to glare at the nurse, who kept smiling at Jack like she was starving and he was strawberry cheesecake.

"I'll be back in a few, and then I want to head out to Dave's place and see what I can see," he said, his face grim.

"I'll probably go with you. There are plenty of people here who want to see Dave, and I don't need to add to the crowd. He's probably tired and woozy now, anyway, and just wants to sleep."

He touched my arm and then followed the nurse out of the room. I sat down on a hideously uncomfortable orange chair and prepared to wait, but just then the elevator doors opened. I blew out a sigh of relief at the familiar uniform.

The sheriff of Dead End, Susan Gonzalez, was here now. She'd figure this out.

She scanned the room, nodded to the group still clustered by the vending machine, and then caught sight of me and started across the room. I stood and waited, silently offering up thanks, yet again, that our previous sheriff was long gone and probably locked up in a hole in the ground, never to be seen in Dead End again.

Susan was a friend. A couple of years older than me, she was a little shorter, but had an air of absolute authority and competence which went a long way to making her great at her new job. She had long, silky black hair that she always wore up in a tight bun for work, and her golden eyes and golden-brown skin combined to make her a true beauty in a way most of us could only dream of.

And she was tough as nails.

"Tess, what do you know?"

She was also a "skip the small talk, get straight to the point" person.

"Not much, to be honest. Somebody shot Dave. A man at his company office. Nobody seems to know who or why. Dave jumped out the window, head first, according to the doctor, which is why he only got shot in the ... um ... behind."

Susan blinked. "Is he okay? I mean, clearly he isn't okay, but how bad is it?"

"Not bad, Dr. Boston said. Evidently they only had to clean and suture it, and they're keeping him overnight for observation, but he can go home tomorrow. He'll probably need a pillow or bag of frozen peas, though." I grimaced at the thought of sitting down after you'd been shot in the butt.

Susan wrote something down on the small pad of paper she'd pulled out of a pocket, and then she looked up at me. "Getting shot is no fun, even if it doesn't hit anything vital," she said flatly, and I wondered how she knew—if she'd been shot—but before I could reply, she nodded. "He's probably going to be the butt of a lot of jokes, though."

I groaned. "That was bad. Really, really bad."

She grinned at me. "Yeah, but I almost had to say it." She put her notebook back in her pocket, her smile fading. "I need to talk to Dave. Can he have visitors yet?"

"Yeah, Jack and Eleanor are back there with him. If you go up to that desk, somebody will take you back, I'm sure, although they said only two visitors at a time."

"They'll let me in. Thanks, Tess."

When the nurse opened the doors for Susan, Jack walked out, and they stopped in the doorway to talk, but by the time I crossed the room, they'd finished their conversation.

Jack still looked angry, but his eyes had gone back to green. "Are you ready to go?"

"Yeah. Mike and Ruby are on their way. I should get back to the shop. They'll let me know what's going on and take care of Eleanor."

Jack stopped to tell Julio that Dave would like to see him next.

"He's really going to be okay?" Julio's normally cheerful expression was gone, replaced with a fierce wariness.

"Yeah. He's doped up now, but not too bad. He's still making sense, but a little woozy. I think he wants to talk to you about handling things at work."

"Of course. He knows he doesn't need to worry about that." He started toward the nurse who was patiently waiting next to the open doors and then turned back to Jack. "You're going to find the son of a bitch who did this?"

"Count on it." The ice in Jack's voice must have reassured Julio, who nodded. "Let me know if you need any help."

Jack nodded, and then he headed for the exit marked STAIRS. I could tell without asking that he was too on edge to want to be trapped in an elevator, and I couldn't blame him.

When we started down, the stairwell empty but for us, I touched Jack's shoulder. "What did he say?"

"Not here."

I waited until we were back in the truck, heading out of the parking lot, before I asked again. "What did he say?"

Jack shot me a narrow-eyed glance that promised pain and vengeance. "He didn't know."

"What do you mean, he didn't know? He at least saw him, so he can do a sketch with a police artist, right?"

Jack laughed, but there was no humor in it. "Sure, but he won't tell me anything. Well, almost nothing."

I waited, but he didn't elaborate.

"Okay, enough with the mysterious. Who was it, and why did he shoot Dave? Is it some big misunderstanding? A meth head? An unsatisfied construction customer? Although Dave does such good work, I can't imagine it's that."

Jack said nothing.

I narrowed my eyes and pulled out the big guns. "Fine, if you don't want to talk. We're only thirty miles from home. I guess I'll sing."

I snapped on the radio.

Jack turned pale.

And then he talked.

3

Here's the thing about my singing.

It's ... not great.

I've been told that small children have run screaming just from hearing it. This is somewhat hurtful, but possibly true.

Hence, the threat to Mr. Superior Tiger Hearing.

"He sounds like hired muscle," he said quickly, glancing at me and snapping off the radio. "Talked about moving into town. Starting partnerships. Dave said he didn't need a partner, and the guy pulled out a gun."

"Really?" I rolled my eyes. "Why would anybody try that here? If they do any research at all, they'd know Dead Enders would never work with outsiders who pulled crap like that."

"Maybe it's gang stuff."

"Gangs? Really? We're not exactly a hotbed of crime and money. Even the Dead End Senior Bingo night's biggest haul is two hundred dollars and a case of Granny Josephine's pickled green tomatoes."

Jack whistled. "A whole case? That's almost enough to make me take up bingo. I love those tomatoes."

"That's right, you played football with her grandson in high school, didn't you?"

He grinned and took the exit to Dead End. "Yes, and when we knew Granny Josephine would be cooking dinner for the team, we played our hearts out."

"Did you eat as much then as you do now?"

"I don't eat that much now."

"Ha! You eat as much as a small country! Speaking of which, can we have lunch now? It's almost twelve. We can let everybody at Beau's know Dave is going to be all right."

For maybe the first time since I'd known him, Jack turned down food. "No. I want to get over to Dave's now and find out what's going on."

"Then I'm going with you."

He shot me a raised-eyebrow glance. "Like hell you are. Who knows what may be waiting for me there?"

"Then you shouldn't go there, either! Let Susan and her deputies handle it," I tried, knowing even as the words came out of my mouth that he wouldn't.

Jack said nothing, just shook his head slightly, and we drove the rest of the way to the pawnshop in silence. Before I got out of the truck, though, I paused and put a hand on his arm.

"I know you feel like you have to do this yourself, because you were a soldier, rebel commander, and the biggest, baddest in every situation, but ..." I took a deep, shaky breath. "Just remember that you matter to me. And don't get yourself shot, in the butt or anywhere else."

"That's a clown," he said, staring straight ahead and turning off the ignition.

"What? What does that mean? You think it's clownish of me to care about you? I don't—"

He reached out and gently pushed my chin to the side, until I was facing the windshield, too.

"Oh." I blinked. "It's a *clown*."

Because a clown, in full-on circus attire, was staring into the window of my pawnshop.

And he wasn't alone.

Jack's eyes widened. "It's actually four, no, five, no ... six ... did *seven* clowns really just walk out of that VW Bug?"

"There's a VW van behind it. Some came from there," I pointed out.

"Huh."

We sat for a moment, watching, as seven clowns--red noses, giant rubber shoes, and all—gathered on the porch and milled around, chatting amongst themselves.

"This," I finally said, "is a weird damn day."

"You take the clowns, I'll go check out Dave's office?"

I sighed. "Fine. But you call me the second you ... well, the second you anything. Okay?"

"Deal. Did you hear about the two cannibals who were eating the clown?"

I stopped, hand on the door handle, and stared at him. "What?"

Jack flashed me a brilliant smile. "One said to the other, 'does this taste funny to you?'"

I groaned all the way up to my porch, where a bunch of clowns turned and looked at me.

The one closest to me, a guy wearing a blue and white suit, blue shoes, and a blue wig, pointed at me. "Do you work here?"

"I do. I'm Tess. Sorry for the delay in opening. Welcome

to Dead End Pawn." I unlocked the door, and then the blue clown held it open and waved his hand with a flourish.

"After you, please, Miss."

"I, um, thanks." I was trying to be calm about the fact that seven clowns were trooping into my pawnshop. To be honest, though, after the news about my dad, and then Dave getting shot, the clowns seemed almost anticlimactic.

"What do you call it when a clown holds the door open for you?" A female clown in a mostly orange suit asked me as she filed in.

"Um ..."

"A nice jester!" They all called out the answer at the same time, except for a guy in green who rolled his eyes and sneered at the rest of them. (They all had specific colors to their ensembles, except for a little guy at the back who was geared up in a rainbow of hues.)

I smiled politely, but 'nice jester' wasn't nearly as funny as the cannibal joke, not that I'd ever tell *Jack* that. "How can I help you?"

"We'd like to pawn things," Orange said, shoving her way through the crowd.

The crowd of clowns.

Heh.

Like a pride of lions or a murder of crows? I started to ask but decided against it. Oddly enough, these clowns didn't seem like they had much of a sense of humor.

"Well, you came to the right place," I said as brightly as possible, considering the day I'd had. "We take things in pawn. We're a pawnshop."

I snapped my mouth shut before I said 'yes, indeedy' or something equally stupid and instead just gave them an inquisitive look, simultaneously wondering how Dave was doing, how Eleanor was holding up, if Jack were safe, and why in the world seven clowns in full costume had decided to show up in my shop.

"You can say it, you know," Blue said in a sour tone. "We're used to it."

I looked around, but none of them would meet my gaze. "Ah, I can say what, exactly?"

"What's a clown like you doing in a place like this?" Orange said.

A guy in all red, except for a vividly purple wig, gave me a sad smile. "If you're ever attacked by a gang of clowns, you should go straight for the *juggler.*"

My head started to hurt. "I don't actually—"

"When a clown retires, he leaves some big shoes to fill," Green said glumly.

"OKAY," I said, way too loudly, when I caught Blue opening his mouth, undoubtedly to tell me another teeth-grittingly awful clown joke. "I wasn't going to say any of those things, although of course I'm interested in why you're all here and in costume. But I've had kind of a rough morning, so could we please just skip to what you want to pawn?"

They all gaped at me like I'd stepped on a kitten. By Southern standards, I kind of had. We don't get right to the point in the South as much as we meander around it, until one or the other side caves and asks for a glass of sweet tea.

Aunt Ruby would be so disappointed in me.

Or maybe not. The one time we ran into a clown in public, tying balloon animals at a buffet restaurant, she'd told him to back away from the crying child (me) or she'd tie his *ears* into a balloon animal.

"Nobody likes us anymore," Orange said.

"We blame Stephen King," Blue pitched in, his whole face drooping.

Or maybe that was just his makeup.

"I'm ... sorry. But—"

"Yeah, yeah. We'd like to pawn our ukuleles. Business is down, bookings are waaaaaay down, especially since that *It* movie came out—"

"I loved that movie," Purple said.

Everybody else gasped. I think even I gasped. "Really?"

"Traitor!" Orange accused.

Purple narrowed his eyes and glared at us. "Did you even see the movie?"

I held up my hands and shook my head. "Nope. Not me. Way too scary for me. I've only gone to one scary movie in my entire life, and I started shaking and wanting to cover my eyes."

"That's normal enough," Red graciously conceded.

I sighed. "Yeah, but I was still in the popcorn line. I'm just not made for scary stuff."

"So you hate us, too," Blue put in mournfully.

"No! No, I don't hate clowns! I think you're awesome," I said, exaggerating enormously, but the poor clowns just seemed to need some encouragement. "So. You said ukuleles? We don't get much call for ukuleles, actually. More guitars and—"

Blue pulled a case out of what must have been a giant pocket in his clown suit and gently placed it on my counter. The other six followed suit, until I had a line of seven ukulele cases lined up on the shining glass. As one, they all flipped the latches, opened the lids, and stepped back, so I was presented with a line of glowing wooden ukuleles, seemingly all in pristine condition, which meant they were worth ...

I didn't have a single clue what they were worth.

"Okay. So, first, I need to establish a value," I began, and Blue put a file folder bulging with papers on the counter.

"Bills of sale, comp sales on eBay, descriptions of each one, etc., etc.," he said. "They're soprano ukuleles made of koa wood, which, as you know, is the best wood for optimal tones."

I did not in fact know this. I didn't even know there was a type of wood called koa, or that there were soprano ukuleles. Surprisingly enough, people who work in pawnshops don't automatically know everything about everything in the world. We just do a lot of rapid-Googling. We also are rock stars at trivia games. (Ask me what year the first grandfather clock was created, I dare you.)

"They're worth five thousand dollars each. We'll take checks, but we prefer cash," Orange said.

I blew out a breath. "Did you know the first grandfather clock was created in 1680?"

They all looked confused.

(A crowd of confused clowns clustering around my counter, all of them wearing red rubber noses, is a sight that will more than likely live on in my nightmares for years to come.)

"Never mind. Okay, let me tell you a bit about how pawn shops work."

They all nodded, and even looked mildly interested, as much as I could tell beneath the makeup. Speaking of the makeup ...

"Why are you in full clown costume? I mean, do you walk around like that all the time?"

Blue sighed. "No, Miss—"

"Tess."

"No, Tess, we're on the way to a performance. At a Children's Hospital, in fact."

Now I felt like a terrible person for not being able to give charitable, benevolent clowns top dollar for their ukuleles.

It did not escape my attention that my life was getting weirder by the minute.

"Oh. I'm sorry. I won't hold you up. But here's how the pawn business works: we specialize in short-term loans for people who don't have the kind of collateral that banks demand. You probably know this, right?"

They all nodded. Green shot a stream of water out of a flower on his lapel at Purple, who pulled a rubber bat out of a pocket and bopped Green over the head with it.

I assumed that meant "Yes, we get it, move on, already," so I moved on.

"Most of those people come back for their property, after making the loan plus interest payments. Is that what you want? The other option is maybe I could buy a couple of them outright. The problem is that there's not much of a market in Dead End for used ukuleles, even such fine ones as these." I did not want to buy ukuleles, but these were clowns who were performing at a children's hospital, and what kind of monster wouldn't help them out?

They stared at each other in silence, a couple of them scuffing their enormous shoes on my floor, and I tried not to think about whether they were leaving marks and how hard it would be to clean them off the floors, but when you are the business owner and the business janitor all rolled up into one person, it's hard not to think about these things sometimes.

And those were some very big shoes.

"Yes. Maybe. If we pawn them and don't ... *can't* ... come back for them, what happens?"

I bit my lip and tried not to feel like a horrible person. "Then you forfeit your items—your ukuleles—and I put them up for sale to recoup my expenses."

They drooped, and I realized I'd hit a new low.

I'd made clowns sad.

The starting notes of *Tears of a Clown* started rolling through my head, and I managed to stop myself from bashing my head against the wall, but it took some doing.

Finally, Blue looked around at them all, and some silent communication must have occurred, because then he nodded. "Okay. We'll pawn them, or as many as you'll take, but we'll definitely come back for them. How's that?"

Nobody looked like they were starting to cry, so I considered that a win and smiled. "Okay. But I need to do a bit of research. Can I offer you some water?"

A few minutes later, they all had bottles of water and were browsing the shop while I reviewed their file and did some research on my own. None of it made me any happier about the idea of taking ukuleles. As much as I despised the thought, I was going to suggest they consider my competition.

"I realize these are very valuable to you, but I have to run a business based on what I think I can sell an item for, minus the overhead, like my mortgage payment, electricity, what I pay my employee, taxes, etc. Does that make sense?"

They nodded, but they didn't look happy about it. No tears, though, thankfully.

"It's like the circus," I said, grasping for inspiration. "Somebody may pay ten dollars for a ticket, but all of that doesn't go to the performers, right?"

"We get how business works," Orange said dryly. "Don't judge us on our pretty faces."

"Right. Sorry. Basically, it boils down to this: I can't really give you anywhere near the five thousand each. In fact, since you mentioned eBay, why don't you try there? That's a much more likely spot for a, um, ukulele aficionado to look for one than in my little pawnshop in tiny Dead End, Florida." I had a love/hate relationship with eBay, which had come close to putting pawnshops out of business there for a while, but sometimes I was forced to recommend it.

A situation with seven clowns and seven ukuleles was—definitely—exactly such a situation.

"Can you take even a few of them? See how it goes?" Green looked hopeful enough that I bit my lip and wondered how much I could afford to offer for one or even two of them. I mean, compared to the Jackalope ...

"Well, if I—"

The bells over my door tinkled, and the clowns and I all looked up to see a handsome, slim man with graying blond hair take a step into the shop and freeze.

"Tess, why are there a bunch of clowns in your shop?"

"They're looking for their rubber chickens," I shot back, determined to be calm, as the one person I did not want to face on my own walked back into my life.

The clowns started clapping.

"Good one, Tess," Blue said. "Looking for their rubber chickens. I *love* it."

Orange whistled her approval, and a few of the others stamped their overly large feet and grinned at me.

I appreciated the applause, but I was too focused on my new visitor to pay much attention. Instead, I clenched my hands into fists behind my back and tried to keep from letting anyone see me tremble. "Why are you here, *Dad*? I mean, you haven't bothered to call, or write, or visit, or even send me a damn postcard since you walked out on me when I was three years old, so why now?"

Okay. So much for calm.

"*Dad*?" Red folded his arms across his beach-ball-sized belly. "You abandoned your own daughter?"

Suddenly, the mood in the shop—and the actual positions of everyone in it—shifted, and it was me and seven clowns facing my long-lost father. The soundtrack in my skull switched from *Tears of a Clown* to *The Magnificent Seven.*

"Looks like you have some 'splaining to do, Lucy," Orange offered.

"And some apologizing," Blue said, scowling at my long-lost father.

Green nodded and pulled off his rubber nose and dropped it into a pocket. "Maybe we should all sit down and discuss this. I'm sure Tess and her father have some feelings they need to get out on the table."

This was not how I'd envisioned my day going when I got out of bed this morning. Note to self: stay in bed next time. Still, I stayed silent. Not that I needed clowns to stand up for me, but I'd said what I needed to say.

"I'm not going to discuss my daughter with, no offense, a bunch of clowns," my father said, his Irish brogue rolling into the tension in the room, more pronounced than I remembered, but, then again, I'd been three the last time I'd heard his voice. He could have sounded like the Lucky Charms leprechaun, for all I knew.

Red pointed a long, polka-dotted, gloved finger at my father. "What are you, some kind of bigot? Clowns have feelings, too."

My father scanned the room, his lips tightening, and then he forced a smile. "What do you say, Dumpling? Can you spare a few minutes alone with your dad? For old times' sake?"

That did it. *Old times' sake,* my ass.

"We don't *have* any old times, *Thomas*, and that's all on you. Now, if you'll excuse me, I have customers. Perhaps you could come back another time," I said, with so much ice in my voice I nearly froze my tongue.

Holding on to my composure by the thinnest of threads.

I would *not* break down and cry in front of a bunch of clowns, no matter how nice they were. And I absolutely would not cry one tear in front of the man who threw me out like I was garbage. Abandoned me and never came back.

Never communicated in any way.

"You should leave, buddy," Purple said. "Don't make us go all *It* on your ass."

My father's brows drew together in obvious confusion, but I wasn't going to explain pop culture to him.

"All right, Dumpling—"

"*Don't* call me that." He'd lost the right to any pet names more than twenty long years ago.

"All right. Tess," he said quietly. "I'm sorry. I'll be at Mike's. Please come over when you can. We need to talk."

Those hideous four words again.

We all watched him walk out the door, and then my energy disappeared, and I collapsed onto the stool I kept behind my counter.

"Well. That was like clowns in a circus," Green said, blowing out a huge breath.

I just gaped at him for a moment, and then I got it. "Intense. In *tents*. Like clowns in a circus. I get it." I started laughing, more and more hysterically, and then I burst into tears.

When Jack walked in ten minutes later, I was crying and surrounded by clowns.

That's when things *really* got weird.

4

Jack took one look at me and the clowns surrounding me and then shifted. One moment the hottest guy I'd ever met was standing in the door-way, and the next moment, a quarter ton of Bengal tiger was leaping across the shop in a single bound.

Like a furry, snarling, Super Tiger.

Clowns scattered like rainbow-colored bowling pins. Blue, though, was made from sterner stuff, and he grabbed one of the ukuleles and crouched, holding the instrument overhead like a baseball bat or a sword, putting himself between me and the oncoming tiger.

It was one of the bravest things I've ever seen.

And, okay, one of the funniest.

"Stay away," Blue shouted, brandishing the ukulele. "I won't let you harm her."

Jack leapt over Blue's head, the counter, and me, and landed behind me. Then he immediately pushed his enor-mous furry body between me and the rest of the room, shoving me, stool and all, back against the wall.

Then he roared so loudly that the walls shook.

If you've ever heard a tiger roar, you know that I'm not exaggerating when I say that all the clowns in the shop started running, crying, screaming, or some combination of the three. Even courageous Blue faltered, his throat working as he swallowed, hard.

Okay. That was enough. Bad enough I nearly made clowns cry, now Jack was scaring the crap out of them. I wiped my cheeks with the back of my hands and stood, shoving at Jack's shoulder to move him out of the way. Jack being Jack, this had absolutely zero effect on him.

"Enough!"

When he continued snarling at my clowns, er, my customers, I flicked his ear to get his attention. "They're customers. I was crying because I'm an idiot, and my father was here, not because of them. Now, shift back and say you're sorry."

Six of the clowns' mouths fell open, and they stared at me in utter shock.

The seventh clown fainted in a puddle of purple silk.

"Now look what you've done," I scolded Jack, who gave a sheepish swish of his tail and then, in a shimmer of silvery magic, shifted back to human. Fully clothed human, thankfully, because a few of the clowns' expressions shifted, as well, from terrified to intrigued.

Jack has that effect on people.

He ignored them all, though, and turned his focus to me. "Why were you crying? What did your father do?"

"He called her Dumpling!" Orange said, hands on hips. "After he *abandoned* her when she was a baby."

"Well, I was three—"

"Three is a baby," she snapped. "What a horrible man."

Jack put an arm around me and gave me a brief hug, and I think he whispered something into my ear, but it sounded like "only you, Tess," so I chose to ignore him. I pushed him away and took a deep breath, then I realized we were still one clown down.

"Shouldn't we do something about Purple?"

"Who?" Green looked around. "Oh. Melvin. Yeah. He does that. He's like the human version of a fainting goat."

"Tess has an earless goat," Jack offered, which was the weirdest apology I'd ever heard, but apparently the clowns were willing to let his dramatic entrance go, because they started plying him with questions about goats, ignoring Purple—Melvin—until I sighed again and went over to my fallen potential customer and shook him gently, helped him sit up, and gave him a bottle of water.

Melvin took a long drink and then pointed to Jack. "That's Jack Shepherd," he called out, in a loud and somewhat dramatic voice. "Jack. Shepherd. Remember Cleveland? *That* Jack Shepherd."

The clowns all froze and went completely silent. Seven pairs of extremely made-up eyes and one pair not wearing any makeup at all (mine) turned to stare at Jack.

"No! Not *Cleveland*," Blue said in a hushed tone. "Him?"

Purple pushed out his lip and frowned. "Know any other tiger shifters?"

Orange raised one orange-striped, gloved hand and covered her mouth. "No! Really? *Cleveland*?"

"And we all know what happened there," Green intoned, nodding his head somberly.

I raised a hand. "I don't. I don't know what happened there."

The clowns said nothing.

Jack said nothing.

I wanted to strangle somebody, but the potential headline stopped me:

LOCAL PAWNSHOP OWNER STRANGLES CLOWNS ON THEIR WAY TO PERFORM AT CHILDREN'S HOSPITAL

I'd *never* live that down.

"What happened in Cleveland?" My voice was just a touch shrill, even I could hear it, but it had been a long, long day.

"We can never speak of Cleveland," Purple said, pushing himself up off the floor. "It's a sacred clown trust."

Yet another expression I'd never thought I'd hear in my pawnshop: "sacred clown trust."

"Well, then." I rolled my eyes. "Let's forget all this and look at the ukuleles. I think I can take two of them ..."

"What ukuleles?" Jack, standing directly in front of the counter where the seven ukuleles rested in their cases, asked.

I raised an eyebrow.

He glanced down. "Oh. Those ukuleles. Are you buying them?"

The clowns perked up, hope shining beneath their makeup.

Great. I get to crush the hopes and dreams of kind-hearted clowns. Thanks, Jack.

"I can only take two of them, I think," I began, because I really, really didn't see how I'd unload even two of them, but I wasn't willing to send my clowns off empty-handed.

Jack aimed a direct look at Blue. "Why do you need the money?"

"Jack! We don't ask customers why they need money. It's none of our business," I said, scandalized. Poor Jeremiah would have been appalled.

"Bookings are way down, and we need some new costumes and equipment to have a chance to be part of a great new performance circus starting up in Tampa," Blue said matter-of-factly. "We'd hoped to be able to get twenty grand in seed money with the ukuleles, but it's looking like that won't happen."

"And we're going to be late," Orange put in anxiously, looking at the enormous watch on her wrist.

Jack looked a question at me, so I explained about the children's hospital.

"I'll buy three of them," I said, resigning myself to eating mac and cheese for a month or two. Ramen noodles, maybe. They were five for a buck.

"Don't you guys need them to perform?" Jack shoved his hands in his pockets and leaned against the counter, the picture of nonchalance, in spite of 1) Cleveland, whatever *that* was about, and 2) the fact that he was sticking his giant tiger nose into my business.

But it would have been rude to argue with him in front of the customers, so I just held my breath and silently counted to ten.

1, 2, 3 ...

"I'll give you the twenty grand for the seed money," Jack said, shrugging. "And I'll make a donation to the hospital, too. No worries."

4, 5, 6, 7. Oh, no, he didn't, 8, 9, 10

7,000 ...

The counting wasn't working.

"Jack," I said, smiling sweetly. "May I speak to you in the back?"

The clowns frowned at me. "Are you hurt? Why are you grimacing like that?"

Orange started rummaging in the satchel she carried. "I bet it's constipation. I can recognize that look from a mile away. I have some medicine in here ..."

"No!" I shouted. "It's not consti—I wasn't grimacing, I was smiling sweetly, and—"

"Oh, honey, no," Purple said, making a tsking sound. "That was a grimace."

"Trust us, we know faces," Green added. "Like this—" he contorted his face into a hideous, terrifying expression. "That's what you looked like. Seriously, you could work with us."

"Or be in the next *It* movie," Purple helpfully added. "You wouldn't even need much makeup."

"Thank you very much, " I gritted out. "I believe Jack and I are going to have a chat—"

"In a minute, Tess," Jack said. He strode through the connecting door and into his office, and I spent a happy minute or so contemplating all the ways I was going to beat him to death with his own tail, or with my new Jackalope, but before I could conquer my new, murderous tendencies or even think of something to say to the clowns, he was back, holding two pieces of paper that looked a lot like business checks.

"Hospital's name?"

They told him, and he wrote something on one.

"Your name?"

Turns out Blue was Bob Galianakis.

Jack scribbled something on the second.

"Here you go," he said, handing the two checks to Blue. "It's the least I can do."

Blue took the checks, stared at them, and then I almost could have sworn he turned pale beneath his clown makeup. "You ... you're just giving us twenty-five thousand dollars? And another twenty-five to the hospital? I don't—we can't accept—how--"

Jack shrugged, looking like he wanted to be anyplace

else. He wasn't good at accepting thanks or, apparently, hero worship from clowns.

All of them crowded around to see the checks and then to pour even more thanks on Jack, making him squirm, but, in a surprisingly short amount of time, he gathered their contact information, gave them his card, and nudged them out the door—ukuleles in hand—so they wouldn't be late for the hospital.

I, on the other hand, pretty much just stood, speechless, watching all of this with a rather considerable amount of shock, until all seven clowns came up to hug me goodbye before they left.

"You're the best, Tess. Don't let your father push you around," Orange whispered when she hugged me. Before I could think of a response, they were gone.

Jack walked them out, and when he came back in, I was still standing there, mouth hanging open.

He took one look at me and stopped. "Are you okay? None of them touched you with bare skin, did they?"

Jack knew about my ... gift.

"No. Well, except Purple, and he's going to die when he's very old, surrounded by his friends at a clown convention." I blinked. "It's not that. I don't--What just happened? Did you actually just give fifty thousand dollars to a bunch of clowns you've never seen before?"

He shrugged, and I almost could have sworn he blushed. "Technically, I only gave them half that. The rest was for the hospital."

"But ... but ... I mean, money for the hospital, that's wonderful, but what ... how ..."

"I kind of had to do it, Tess. A clown saved my life once."

5

"Nope." I closed my eyes, shook my head, and marched over to the front door, passing Jack on the way. He was smart enough to move out of the way, or I probably would have run him down. "Nope, nope, nope."

"Nope?"

I turned the OPEN sign to CLOSED. "*Nope.* Nope, I'm not asking about how a clown saved your life, or how flying monkeys attacked you in Japan, or how you helped save Atlantis. I'm not asking about Cleveland, or rebel forces, or how you once fought a saber-toothed tiger in Sedona. I'm done playing the comedic sidekick when you drop these nuggets of insanity about your life during the past ten-plus years. So, nope to that and yes to lunch. Do you want to go with me, or would you rather stay here, handing out wads of money to passing circus performers?"

I had to stop talking, because I ran out oxygen, and frankly, I'd said more than enough.

"Tess." A slow, sexy, smile spread across his face, and he started to saunter toward me.

"Nope. Lunch or not? Last chance?"

"Tess. Of course I want to have lunch with you. And, honey?"

"Don't call me honey," I muttered, echoes of *Dumpling* running through my brain.

He pushed a strand of hair behind my ear and leaned close. "You're nobody's sidekick."

Stupid tiger shifters and their stupid sexy voices.

I told my lady parts to calm the heck down, locked the door behind us, and we went to Beau's.

"I'm driving," I told him, heading over to my beautiful new Mustang. "No arguments."

He grinned and held up his hands. "None here."

"Good."

On the way to Beau's, Dead End's only sit-in restaurant, Jack texted Eleanor for an update.

"He's doing fine, but his energy *bottomed* out, and he's sleeping now," Jack reported.

I rolled my eyes. "Are you going to get tired of butt jokes any time soon?"

"I doubt it, but I'll let you know." He leaned over to turn on the radio, glanced at me, and hastily let his hand drop.

"You're not funny," I told him.

"I'm a little bit funny."

"Did Dave tell you anything else? What the guy wanted? More about what happened?"

"No." Jack's jaw tightened. "He wouldn't tell me much. I got the feeling he was trying to protect me from going after the people who hurt him. And I didn't see anything at Dave's office. No note labeled CLUE or anything."

"Dave wanted to protect you."

Jack growled, deep in his throat. "He's pure human, and he has a kid. It's my job to protect *him*."

Okaaaay. Time to change the subject.

"Are you going to tell me about Cleveland on our ... date?" Which was only two days away. *Argh*. I hadn't thought about it being Thursday when I'd said Saturday.

"I can't. Sacred clown trust, remember?"

"You're so annoying, you do realize that, right?" I slowed to a stop at the crosswalk in front of the bank to let Sally DeSario push her wagon of toddlers to the park. The wagon was painted bright red, with DEAD END DAYCARE written on the side in block letters.

Sally wasn't much taller than the wagon; maybe four feet tall at the most. Her chestnut brown skin gleamed in the sun, and her long, brown braid was tied with bright red ribbons. She smiled at something one of the children said, waved to me, and headed on toward the park in the center of town.

"There were eight children in that wagon," Jack said slowly. "And only one person to supervise them?"

"She's a Brownie." I put on my turn signal to turn into the parking space.

"What does her name matter?"

I glanced at him, but he wasn't kidding. "Oh. You don't know. I forget sometimes how long you've been gone. Sally's *name* isn't Brownie, it's DeSario. She *is* a Brownie. She could handle twice that number of kids at the park. They listen to everything she says, because they all adore her."

Jack's eyes narrowed. "Brownies are terrific for cleaning houses and doing the mending, but watching kids?"

"I don't know about all Brownies, but she certainly is. We don't stereotype based on species here, Jack. This is Dead End. You should know that by now. We knew supernatural beings existed since long before they came out to the general public back in 2006."

"What happens when her natural inclination to cause mischief takes over?"

"Mischief?" I grinned at him. "Did you really just say *mischief*?"

"It's in the *Basic Handbook of Creatures Formerly Known as Mythical* we gave all incoming rebel soldiers," he muttered. "Chapter 37."

Of course he knew the chapter number.

"And what did the basic handbook say about tiger shifters?"

Jack's smile suddenly had much sharper teeth. "One word: Beware."

I started laughing, and we got out of the car. "Should have been two words: Giant Ego."

When we were out of the car, though, my momentary good mood fled. I turned and faced Jack over the hood.

"My father said he'd be at Uncle Mike's. Am I being a coward? Should I go see what he wants now and get it over with?"

Jack walked around the car and took my hand. "Why would you possibly rush to see him, after he's made you wait all this time? To hell with him. Let's have a nice lunch and figure out our next steps."

Just then, the Peterson brothers walked out of Beau's, on their way back to Dead End Hardware, no doubt, and the scent of fried onions wafted out, convincing my empty stomach that this was the best plan.

"Deal."

"Hello, young man," one of the Misters Peterson (I could never tell them apart; they both had gray hair, gray beards, and a wardrobe that consisted of overalls, overalls, overalls, and flannel shirts) said to Jack. "How is that floor refinishing coming along?"

"Not bad, sir," Jack said, nodding. "That sander you rented me works like a charm. I'm glad I didn't buy the cheaper version."

"Quality always tells," the other brother proclaimed, grasping the straps of his overalls and rocking back on the heels of his scuffed work boots.

"Quality does, quality does," his brother echoed. Their attention turned to me. "You've done a good job carrying on after we lost Jeremiah, young lady. You ever need any business advice, you come to us, you hear? We've been running a store since Christ was a corporal, and we'd be glad to help out."

Suddenly, my throat was tight. My own father may abandoned me, but my Dead End neighbors were always ready to lend a hand. I loved my town. Taken by an impulse I didn't stop to analyze, I leaned in and kissed both brothers on their cheeks.

"That's very kind of you. I will definitely take you up on that. Thank you."

Their faces turned red clear to the tips of their ears, and they made some fierce, throat-clearing sounds, before mumbling goodbyes and escaping.

Jack watched them walk off and then turned to me. "Tess, I swear you could charm the birds out of the trees."

"What would I do with a bunch of birds? Smelly things, bird poo all over the place. Come on, let's eat. I'm starved."

～

*B*eau's Diner was the social center of Dead End, and hostess/waitress/bouncer Lorraine was the social center of Beau's. She was in her seventies and maybe five feet tall in her orthopedic shoes, but it was five feet of pure command. She spotted us in the doorway and headed straight toward us.

"It's about time you two came to visit me. I haven't seen you in forever."

"We were here three days ago," I said dryly.

Jack hugged her. "But I've missed you like it was forever ago, ma'am."

She swatted his arm with the order pad she never used and grinned up at him.

Way, way up, considering the top of her head hit him mid-chest.

"Come on, I'll put you by the window. And be prepared, I'm going to tap both of you to help with hurricane prep later this month."

"We'd be glad to," I told her. Hurricane season in Florida was no joke. It was always all hands on deck, so to speak, in Dead End.

Jack nodded but then glanced around, and his smile vanished. "Sure. And actually, we'd like to be seated over there, next to the mayor."

Lorraine studied Jack's face, shrugged, and then led us over to an empty table against the wall, right next to the mayor's table.

I grabbed Jack's arm and spoke too quietly to be heard over the sounds of forks hitting plates and cheerful lunchtime conversations. "Since when are you interested in politics?"

He leaned down to murmur in my ear. "Since our illustrious Mayor Ratbottom began entertaining the Irish mob."

"I'm surprised you'd let me anywhere near them," I blurted out without thinking.

He sighed. "I've given up. You have the astonishing

ability to land yourself in the middle of trouble—or a herd of alligators—unless I keep an eye on you at all times."

"Hey!" I poked him in the arm. "Those alligators were your fault. You and your swamp commandos. And if that video *ever* shows up on YouTube, you're a dead man."

"I humbly apologize. And I promise you, the video was deleted. Just after I watched it seven or thirty times."

To his credit, he didn't start laughing right there and then, but I could tell he wanted to, so forget about the credit. He was in demerit territory.

We sat down and ordered. Lemonade with extra ice for Jack, plus seven of the chicken-fried steak specials, with extra pie. Coffee and meatloaf for me, with double mashed potatoes instead of the peas.

"I know, you hate cooked peas," Lorraine said, not writing anything down, as usual. "You'll have a side of apple sauce to make up for the lack of vegetables. And pie?"

I took a deep breath and tried to measure how much my jeans' waistband cut into my stomach. "Maybe no pie this time. I'll have a bite of his."

"Hey!" Jack paused in stacking the sugar packets he'd dumped out of their ceramic box. "I barely ordered enough for me."

"You'll survive. Now, what's up?" I attempted a surreptitious side-eyed glance at the mayor and his three guests, and Jack kicked me under the table.

"Ouch! What?"

He leaned across the table. "Stop looking. Also, you really *do* look constipated. Did you take some of that medicine from the clown?"

I narrowed my eyes. "I was trying to be stealthy. And, hey, keep it up with the romantic talk about bowels. It's a great mood-setter for our date."

Lorraine dropped off our drinks, and when I turned to thank her, I realized that one of the guys at the mayor's table was staring at me. Caught off guard, I nodded at him, and he flinched and turned to the man at his right, elbowing him in the ribs.

Then they both stared at me.

This was weird.

"Jack," I hissed. "They're staring at me. What should I do?"

Jack's face hardened, all amusement draining away until he was one hundred percent lethal soldier. I hated that so many situations in Dead End had forced him into battle mode since he'd been back, but I'd been right there with him—and would continue to be—anytime he needed me.

Also, I'd been practicing shooting with the rifle Uncle Mike gave me. I wasn't a dead shot yet, by any means, but I now reliably hit what I aimed at more than 90% of the time from up to twenty-five yards away.

I'd had more than enough reasons, recently, to want to be a better shot.

Now, the Irish mob was in town.

Yes, I'd be doing more target shooting in my near future.

Jack turned in his chair until he was facing the mayor's table. "O'Sullivan. What's scum like you doing in my town?"

The oldest of the three, the one sitting directly across from the mayor and nearest to Jack, barked out a harsh laugh. He was a big man, probably six feet tall and very broad. His thinning reddish hair covered a sunburned scalp, and his wide nose had the look of years of sun, drink, and maybe a bar fight or three.

Noses were not supposed to turn to the left like that.

"Your town, boyo? Last I heard, Ratbottom here was the mayor of this shithole."

"Hey! Dead End is a great town," I said, glaring at him. "Why don't you go back to New York, if you don't like it here?"

O'Sullivan turned his reptilian gaze to me. "How do you know I'm from New York? Did you use your *special power*?"

"No, I listened to your accent." I rolled my eyes in a show of nonchalance, but inside I was not happy. How did he know who I was? My 'special power' had been in the news, but that had been a long time ago. I didn't like the idea that Mr. Mob Boss was singling me out.

"Now, gentlemen. Er, and lady," Mayor Ratbottom bluffed, holding his hands out in a conciliatory gesture. "Let's just eat our lunch and discuss—"

"Shut it, Ronald," O'Sullivan said, his eyes still on me. "We discuss what I want to discuss when I want to discuss it. Why don't you be a good boy and go back to your office?"

The mayor made a blustering noise or two but then scuttled off like the weasel he was. There had been rumors of election fraud when he'd run for mayor, and I was starting to believe them.

"Why are you in town?" Jack's voice was sharp enough to cut glass. "And what do you know about any special *activities* in town this morning?"

O'Sullivan waved a hand dismissively, but the two with him each moved a hand toward their suit jackets. Lorraine and a helper picked that moment to walk between our tables and drop off our mountain of food—tigers eat a *lot*—and then she turned around, whipped a pistol out of her apron pocket, and aimed it at O'Sullivan's head.

"I'd tell your friends that they want to think again about going for those guns," she drawled, part Steel Magnolia and part Wild West gunslinger. "If you look around, you'll see that we don't take kindly to strangers threatening our own in our town."

We all looked around. I could feel an enormous smile practically split my face in half when I saw that almost every person at every table in the place was aiming a weapon at the mob guys. Mrs. Frost even had her miniature crossbow out and drawn.

"I love this town," I called out. "You are all awesome."

The two thugs started sweating, very slowly and carefully moved their hands away from their pockets, and raised them into the air.

O'Sullivan never took his eyes off me. "No problem. We're done here, anyway. Have a nice lunch, now."

They stood. O'Sullivan tossed money on the table and then turned back to me. "I know about you."

I was done being threatened, even indirectly. "Yeah? Why don't you shake my hand, then?"

I held out my hand, and O'Sullivan showed a hint of fear that hadn't been on his face or in his eyes when every gun in the place was pointed at him.

"Not me." He pointed to one of his minions. "You. Shake the girl's hand."

The man's eyebrows drew together, but he shrugged, not looking the least bit nervous. So, he didn't know about me, then. He walked over and held out his hand, but I yanked mine back.

I had no desire to know how this man was going to die. Especially since, considering the company he kept, it would probably be violent.

"Do it," O'Sullivan suddenly spat out, and the man darted forward and grabbed my hand. A fraction of a second later, he was dangling in the air, held up by a large, claw-tipped hand around his neck, and I was fighting to stay upright. Some visions smashed into me with more force others.

But I *would not* show weakness in front of these people.

Jack's face was granite. "If you ever touch her again, you will die. If you even look at her, you will die. Do you understand me?"

The man made choking noises but must have managed to convey his agreement, because Jack released him, and he crumpled to the ground with a thud of his polished shoes, barely managing to stay upright.

Somehow, while this was happening, I managed to grit my teeth and keep from passing out from the vision, but it was touch-and-go for a few moments. Then I flashed my most brilliant smile up at O'Sullivan.

"Happy?

He scowled. "No. What did you see?"

The diner was silent. Everybody in town knew about me.

"You're going to live a long and happy life and die surrounded by family and friends," I told the thug who'd grabbed my hand.

Anybody who knew anything about me knew that I see absolutely zero about how people live their lives. I only see their deaths. I was betting these men hadn't researched me that closely, though. I was just the town oddity, after all.

I blew out a breath. *Enough* with the bitterness and self-pity.

The man I'd just given a fake prediction, though—who was still clutching his neck and making choking noises—whipped his head around to stare at his boss. "This is her? You made me shake *her* hand?"

"And you got good news. You should be happy. We're out of here," O'Sullivan snapped.

"We're going to have a conversation if I run into you

again," Jack said. "Do you know who I am?"

The man he'd grabbed by the neck nodded frantically and backed away. O'Sullivan only smiled. "But do you live up to your reputation? I wonder," he said softly, poison underscoring every syllable.

"If you know what's good for you, you'll leave town now and never come back."

O'Sullivan simply shrugged, but then he turned and walked away, the non-choking member of his group following closely behind, but darting glances over his shoulder at Jack and me. The man who'd grabbed my hand was behind the other two, so when he turned to follow them out of the diner, I held up a hand to stop him. "Look. I don't ... I lied. Just stay out of the middle of any roads, okay?"

His eyes widened until I could see the whites all the way around his pupils. "What? I can't drive?"

"No. Just don't *stand* in any roads. Ever. Okay?"

He gulped, nodded, and then ran out the door.

Jack crouched down in the aisle in front of me and took my hands. "Are you all right?"

I took a long, deep, shaky breath. "Yeah. I don't know why I lied. I just didn't want that horrible O'Sullivan to get any satisfaction out of forcing me to have a vision like that."

"He's not going to die of old age, is he?" Jack squeezed my hands and stood, watching the mob guys through the window.

I shook my head, feeling acid rising up my throat. "No. No, he's going to get hit—"

"By the Dead End Dairy truck?"

"What? How—"

The squeal of brakes and a loud *thud* interrupted whatever I'd been about to ask, and I shoved back my chair to stand and look out the front window.

The dairy truck was stopped at a crazy angle in the middle of the street, and the man whose death I'd foreseen lay in a crumpled heap on the road ten feet away.

My knees went weak, and I caught myself with a hand on the table before I fell.

"Nope," I whispered. "Nope, nope, nope."

"Tess?" Jack's strong arm was around me, supporting me.

"I would very much like to go home now," I said, knowing he'd hear me even over the din of everybody in the diner who'd seen the accident. "I've had enough of today."

When we left the diner, everyone who wasn't staring at the accident scene stared at me.

Like I'd had something to do with it.

"I only *see* them, I don't *cause* them," I said loudly into the sudden silence, my voice shaky. "You know that, right?"

"Of course we know that," Lorraine said, glaring around the room. Most people found something else to look at, fast.

She patted my arm, which was fine, because I'd first touched Lorraine's hand long ago and discovered she was one of the people, thankfully, whose death I did not see. "I'll pack up your lunches and send them along," she told us. "Your house, Tess?"

Jack looked at me for the decision.

"Yes. I'm just done for the day. If—when—Susan wants to hear about our conversation with those men, have her call me or come over."

Lorraine nodded and pointed at Jack. "You take care of her, you hear me?"

"Yes, ma'am, I wouldn't want to be put to washing dishes again."

She nodded. "Damn straight."

My car was on the other side of the diner from the accident, and I made a point not to look over at the man lying dead in the road even once.

Jack took the keys out of my hands, which were trembling, and opened the passenger door for me. Then we drove in silence toward my place.

"Tess? Are you okay?"

I laughed, but there was no amusement in it. "No, I'm not okay. Would you be okay, if you'd just seen a man's death—twice? Once in your head, and then once in real time?"

He swore beneath his breath, and his hands clenched on my steering wheel.

"Jack. Don't break my new car." Given his tiger strength, this was an actual possibility.

"Would it help to know that the guy whose death you saw is one of the ones who makes a point to kill a police officer in every new territory they try to take over? He would have gone after Susan or young Kelly, if O'Sullivan's really here to expand."

I blew out a breath. It didn't exactly help ... and yet, it did, a little.

"But he was still a person," I finally said. "And I saw his death. I hate this *so much.*"

He swallowed so hard I could hear the gulping sound, and then he lifted his chin. "If it helps ... if it helps, you can sing along with the radio."

I couldn't help it. I started laughing, and my laughter came perilously close to tears. "And now, enter the apocalypse. Mr. Sensitive Tiger Hearing is willing to listen to me sing."

He reached over and patted my leg. "Well. It's been a weird, damn day."

I very carefully inhaled and exhaled, trying to control my breathing, all the way home.

When we turned onto the short dirt road to my house, the empty house down the road was still deserted, but showed signs of activity. A large construction-waste bin sat in front of it, and a sign that this was a **WOLF CONSTRUCTION PROJECT** sat in front.

"Did Dave tell you who bought the house?" Jack and Dave had been good friends since high school, and I knew they liked to shoot pool and shoot the breeze once a week or so.

"Some guy named Gonzalez."

"Gonzalez? Related to Susan?"

"I don't know. It's a common enough name in Florida." Jack shrugged. "Carlos, maybe?"

"No! Carlos Gonzalez is going to be my neighbor? Oh, boy. Every girl in high school had a crush on him. Mr. Tall, Dark, and Handsome. I'm suddenly going to be getting a lot of female company."

Jack's eyes narrowed. "As I said, it's a common enough

name. This Carlos could be Mr. Short, Squatty, and Hideous."

I sighed. "Yeah, knowing my luck, he's a toad. Or, worse, a toad shifter."

"Tess. There are no toad shifters."

"You said there are snake shifters!"

"Yes. Snakes, not toads."

"Whatever. I don't care. I just want to get in my house, make some tea, and eat the rest of the pecan pie I baked yesterday."

"You have pie?" Jack's eyes gleamed. "You know I love the pecan pie you bake."

"Oh, no. You ate most of the last three I baked. You can keep your big, fat paws off this one."

He parked my car expertly at a ninety-degree angle to my house.

Show-off.

"Tess. I have to come in with you, so I can keep on eye on the pecan pie, er, on you, to be sure you don't have any after-effects." He smiled, but I could see the real concern behind his attempt to help me out by lightening the mood.

Unfortunately, there wasn't much that could accomplish that when I'd just seen a man killed. Twice.

"Sure. Whatever."

Not even the sight of my adorable little house could help me out of the dark cloud looming over me. That man had forced me to touch him, it was true—I hadn't brought any of it on myself.

And still ... he was a person. Maybe he had a family waiting for him. And I ... I ...

"Tess." Jack's hand was warm on mine. "It was not your fault. You know that, right?"

I did know that.

I *did*.

Okay.

I unlocked the house, another new development—I'd rarely bothered to lock doors before the events of the past year or so—and my cat, Lou, came streaking through the room and jumped into my arms.

"Hey, sweet girl," I murmured into her silky gray and white fur. "I'm glad to see you, too."

"You sit, and I'll go get some tea and pie." Jack, who inexplicably was good in the kitchen and even liked to wash dishes, headed down the hall, and I sat on the couch with my cat. Then I remembered my phone, which I'd left plugged into the car's charging cable when we went to Beau's. I kissed Lou's head, put her down on the afghan, and ran out to the car.

When I looked at my phone, I was sorry I hadn't just left it there.

Jack was putting a plate and a mug on the coffee table when I got back inside.

"My phone has been blowing up. I have seventeen text messages and eight missed calls." And no plans to answer any of them until I was good and ready.

"This is why I don't have a phone."

"Jack. You have a phone."

He shrugged. "This is why I don't give people my number."

"*I* have your number."

He handed me the mug. "Drink your tea. And you're not people, you're special."

Then, leaving me there with the warmth from his words spreading through my chest, he ambled back down toward the kitchen, no doubt to put the entire second half of the pie on a plate for himself.

Somehow, I couldn't bring myself to be annoyed.

I drank my tea, ate a piece of pie, and then the delivery from Beau's arrived, and I ate some of my mashed potatoes and watched in awe as Jack worked his way through six orders of chicken-fried steak.

"Only six? Are you feeling sick?"

He grinned. "Well, I did eat the rest of the pecan pie before this got here. I'll save the last one for a snack later."

"Fine. *You* go to the store and get me more supplies. Molly is coming over tonight for a movie marathon, and I promised her pie."

He pointed to the boxes of pie from Beau's.

I pointed at him.

"Tigers don't shop," he grumbled, clearing up the trash.

"Oh, yes, they do. You spend at least a few hundred dollars on meat, alone, at Super Target every week. Tigers shop if they want to eat. Get moving, Buddy."

He really didn't want to leave me alone, with criminals in town who'd shown too much interest in me, but I convinced him that 1) they didn't know where I lived, and it's not like anybody in town would tell them, and 2) I needed some alone time. And a nap.

By the time I got him moving, with my grocery list and the fifty dollars he'd refused to take until I'd threatened him with no more pecan pie, ever again, it was almost two in the afternoon. Molly wasn't coming over till seven, since I usually didn't close the shop until six, but after lying on the couch for a while with my eyes closed and my brain racing, I decided to get up and clean.

Cleaning and baking are my two go-to activities when I'm stressed out. I'm a pretty good cook, nothing fancy, but I really love to bake and do a pretty good job. My pies may look lumpy, and my cakes may be a tiny bit lopsided, but they taste delicious.

Aunt Ruby had let me "help" her cook and bake from the time I'd moved in with her and Uncle Mike, twenty-three years ago, and her patient lessons about flour and sugar and Southern hospitality had settled deep into my bones.

I fed Lou and got to work, and soon my house was filled with the scent of apple pies and the music of movie soundtracks. I was dusting with one hand, vacuuming with the other, and singing along to *Frozen*, when I suddenly realized I wasn't alone.

I whirled around, brandishing my feather duster, only to see Jack, arms filled with grocery bags, standing in my hallway.

This time, *he* was the one who looked constipated.

I snapped off the vacuum and dropped the feather duster. "Jack! Are you okay? What happened?"

I ran over and took a couple of grocery bags. "Talk to me. Is it Dave? What's wrong?"

"No. Dave's fine. Eleanor texted to say he's resting and flirting with a handsome nurse."

"Then what's wrong?" I waited, barely breathing, for his answer. I really could not take *one more thing* today.

"Nothing," he mumbled, ducking past me to head to the kitchen. "Let's put these groceries away."

I ran after him, but then my steps slowed as I came to an unpleasant conclusion.

"Jack."

"Nope." He busied himself unpacking groceries and putting them away. Amazing how well he knew his way around my kitchen.

I tapped my foot. "Jack."

"Nope."

"Were you actually *grimacing* because I was singing?"

He flinched, just a little. "Nope. Maybe."

I shoved the groceries at him. "I can't believe you. My singing is not *that* bad. You're the worst person in the world, Jack Shepherd."

I turned to stomp away, but before I took two steps I heard it. Just barely, because he whispered, but I still heard it.

"*Gotcha*."

I whirled back around. "What? Did you just say *gotcha*?"

He stood there, hands full of bags of flour and sugar, grinning like an idiot. A gorgeous idiot, granted, so I either wanted to smack him or kiss him, but I wasn't sure which.

"I thought if you got angry with me, it might help you deal with the fact that your father is on the way over here. Mike texted me when you didn't answer."

"You ... I ... what?"

His smile faded. "Was that a stupid thing to do? A guy thing? I just didn't want to see you hurting, and I figured angry was better, and—"

I stalked him around my kitchen table, step by step. For once, he was the one backing away. "You're telling me that you decided to make me feel horrible about my singing, so I'd be angry instead of sad?"

He put the groceries on the table and shoved one hand through his hair. "Well. When you put it like that, it sounds bad."

"How *should* I put it?"

My doorbell, which hadn't even been working the last time I checked, rang, and the balloon of annoyance in my brain deflated like a souffle at a door-slamming competition.

"That's him?"

"Probably. Unless you're expecting anyone other than

Molly. That's not the sound of her car." His gaze was warm with sympathy. "And sorry you didn't like my brilliant plan, which turned out not to be so brilliant after all."

"Your stupid plan," I muttered, but my heart wasn't in it. My heart, in fact, was currently somewhere down near my socks.

My dad is here.

The doorbell rang again.

"Do you want me to send him away?" Jack put an arm around my shoulders, and for a moment I wanted so badly to let him do just that.

But I couldn't.

I had too many questions.

And, for the first time in twenty-three years, I was going to get some answers.

I walked over to the door and threw it open.

"Hello, Thomas. Long time, no see."

7

My father, who had a death grip on what looked like a stuffed Donald Duck toy, stared at me as if he were trying to memorize my face, and something in my chest stuttered. He held out his hand, but I flinched away. I did *not* want to know how my dad would die.

His face closed down, and he dropped his hand back to his side. "Are you going to invite me in?"

"I'm not sure," I said honestly, trying to decide how I felt about it. "Where are Uncle Mike and Aunt Ruby? I can't imagine they let you come here by yourself."

His lips flattened. "They don't know. I told them I was heading back to the hotel. It was a ... difficult afternoon."

Probably what a lot of those text messages were about. Should have read them, not that anything could have prepared me for this.

"Tess," Jack said from behind me. "If you want him to go, I'll make him go."

My dad bristled. "I don't think you'll be making me do anything I don't want to do. And just who the hell are you?"

"That's my friend, Jack. Jeremiah's nephew."

"Jeremiah?" He looked puzzled for a moment, but then his face cleared. "Oh, right. He's a friend of Mike's. Owns the pawnshop where you work."

Another stab of pain. This time for the loss of the man I'd loved almost like a father. He and Uncle Mike had been the closest I'd ever come to having one, after all.

"He did own the pawnshop. Now I do. Jeremiah died."

"I'm sorry to hear that, Dum—Tess," he said quietly. He even looked sincere when he said it. But what did I know about how good an actor—a liar—this man was? He was a stranger to me.

And he was still standing on my porch.

I sighed and moved back. "Please come in."

My father followed me into my living room and glanced around, deliberately ignoring Jack. "You have a lovely home, Tess. Warm and cozy. Did Jeremiah leave you this, too?"

Anger drove steel into my backbone. "No, he did not. I bought this house myself. And I painted the walls and sanded the floors and learned how to put tile down on the bathroom floors. Uncle Mike and I do repairs, and we even painted the shutters. I don't depend on people giving me things, Thomas."

He flinched and closed his eyes for a moment. When he opened them, he nodded, taking the hit. "I brought you this." He shoved the stuffed duck at me. "I know you always loved Donald Duck."

"I ... thank you." I forced myself to casually put the duck on the coffee table, instead of clutching it to my chest, which had been my first, bizarre, impulse.

"Maybe someday you could call me Dad again."

"Maybe someday you could act like one," Jack growled.

My father finally acknowledged the tiger in the room.

"And you are who, exactly, to Tess? If you're going to be insulting me in my daughter's home, I think I should have the privilege of knowing."

Jack's green eyes flashed with a hint of hot amber, and I stepped between them before fists or claws started to fly. "Jack, this is my father, Thomas Callahan. Uncle Mike's younger brother. Thomas, as I said before, this is Jack Shepherd. My friend."

They shook hands, each trying to stare the other down, and I abruptly grew impatient with both of them. "Fine. Introductions made. Who wants coffee or iced tea?"

"Do you have any beer?" both of them asked at the same time, before glaring at each other.

I rolled my eyes and headed toward the kitchen. "I don't know. Why don't we go find out."

A few minutes later, we were all seated at the table with beer (them) and sweet tea (me) in front of us. Nobody said anything at first, and then we all spoke at once.

"Thomas—"

"What—"

"Tess—"

I raised a hand. "I'll start. Why are you here now? Uncle Mike said you're in some kind of trouble. Is that why you came?"

"Well—"

Jack interrupted. "He probably needs money."

My father laughed a little wildly. "No. That's actually the one thing I *don't* need. Look, Tess, can we talk without your furry friend here? I have some things I'd like to say to you in private."

My eyes had narrowed at 'furry friend.' "You know who he is?"

"Everybody knows who he is. Law breaker. Vigilante.

Outlaw." He took a sip of his beer and placed the bottle very carefully back on the table. "I'm only surprised Mike lets you associate with him."

"Nobody *lets* me do anything. I pick my own friends. I'm not three anymore, as you may have noticed," I shot back. "And he's none of those things you said. He's a freaking hero who has saved more lives that he'd ever admit."

"I'm no hero," Jack said flatly, leaning forward. "On the other hand, everyone does *not* know who I am. Usually only people in a few very specialized circles do. And since you don't look like law enforcement, you came to the shop in daylight, so you're not a vampire, I *know* you're not a shifter, and you can't possibly be from Atlantis, I'm guessing you belong to the final category."

Thomas's brown eyes iced over, but he said nothing.

"What? Jack, what category are you talking about?" I had a sinking suspicion I knew, though.

"The criminal category. Any connection between you suddenly coming *home* and the Irish mob being here, Mr. Callahan?"

"What?" Unless my dad was secretly an Academy-award-winning actor, he was not faking the shock on his face. "What are you talking about?"

"We met Jimmy O'Sullivan at the diner today. He seemed to be interested in Tess, too. Knew about her ..." Jack shot an apologetic look at me. "Her talent."

"What talent?" But this time, my father's eyes flickered, and he didn't quite meet my gaze. So, he was a liar *and* a child abandoner. Bad start to the tally of his sins.

Jack put his bottle down with a thump on my old wooden farmhouse table. "That was a lie. Your heart started racing. Maybe you should try telling the truth for a change."

"Maybe you should mind your own business. I need to

talk to my daughter," my dad said, each word a block of ice.

"Maybe," I said, standing before they could argue about me anymore, "Maybe the two of you should quit talking about me and around me like I'm *not even here*."

I pointed at Jack. "You. Please leave. Thomas is right, I do need some time with him. Alone."

Jack's face set in hard lines. "I don't—"

"I know," I said firmly. "You don't want to annoy me any further than you already have, especially on a weird-ass day like today. Out. I'll call you later."

He finally, reluctantly, stood. "I'll be patrolling your grounds, in case any *more* Irishmen come calling."

"Fine. Thanks. Whatever. Just go, please."

He surprised me by leaning over and kissing me—a firm, brief press of lips—right there in my kitchen, in front of my dad. "If you need me, just call. I'll hear you."

I nodded. I knew he'd hear me, just like I knew he'd probably hear every word my father and I spoke. But I needed at least the illusion of privacy for this conversation. Two decades of pain were engraved on my heart, and I couldn't unveil that picture in front of Jack.

In front of anybody.

My phone started buzzing insistently with an incoming call, and I shut it off without looking and shoved it in a drawer.

"Probably Uncle Mike, again."

Since I was already standing, I motioned to my father. "We may as well go in the living room and be comfortable."

He drained the last of his beer, as though he needed liquid courage to face me with whatever story he was going to tell—although how any story could make up for how he'd blown up my life, I had no idea—and then followed me into the living room.

I sat on a chair and left the couch for him. I couldn't bear to sit any closer to him when every inch of me was buzzing with vulnerability and the anticipation of more hurt to come.

"Why did you leave?"

He laughed, or at least he made it sound something like a laugh, but there were mountains of built-up pain behind it.

"Sure. Let's start off with an easy question, why don't we?"

He scrubbed his face with the back of his hands, and the gesture caught me off guard. It was one I used myself, frequently enough to know that not everybody did.

My eyes that looked exactly like my mother's and nothing like his. But there was something in his smile...

A curve of his lips that I saw in my mirror every day.

"I left because I fell off the edge of the world when your mother died," he finally said, his voice hoarse. "You look so much like her. This beautiful red hair, and your deep, ocean-blue eyes."

He smiled, but there was real anguish in it. "She was my life, Tess. She was my entire reason for existing. She saved me from the worst sides of my soul, and when she died— when she died, there was nothing left of me to give to you."

I hadn't expected the slashing burn of pain that seared through me at his words. I'd thought, after so long, that I'd be immune to letting him hurt me again.

I'd been wrong.

I clutched a pillow so tightly it was a wonder it didn't explode in a cloud of stuffing, then tossed it to the floor. "So, she was your everything. That means I was your nothing. Well, at least we cleared that up. You can go now."

"No! No, you were not nothing to me. You were *never*

nothing to me." He sat perfectly still, but his eyes were storms of pain and, maybe, regret. I tried not to care.

"But I was weak, and I didn't know how to go on without your mother. Demons that had haunted me for so long came flooding back. I started drinking..." He shook his head. "The Irishman stereotype. It's pathetic. *I* was pathetic. I couldn't take care of you the way you deserved, and I knew Mike and Ruby would. I left you, so you could have a better—"

My hands tightened on Lou, who'd climbed into my lap for comfort, mine or hers, until she made a squeaking noise and jumped down to the floor. I was so furious I was shaking. "Don't you *dare* say it. Don't you dare say that you abandoned me for my own good. So I'd have a better life. Don't you dare try to pretend that there was some selfless martyr instinct at work. You were selfish, and you left me—just after my mother died. How can I ever forgive that?"

"I don't expect you to ever forgive me, Tess." His voice was so quiet I could barely hear it. "I can never deserve your forgiveness. Or any forgiveness from Mike and Ruby. Or from your mother, who would've come back from Heaven herself to be with you, if she could've found a way."

My mother. The thought of her brought another sharp stabbing pain. If I loved someone, they left me. This was the lesson my parents had taught me. If I hadn't had Mike and Ruby, and their selfless, constant love, I could've grown up to be defined by that lesson.

Broken.

Shattered.

Instead, I had a good life. I needed to focus on that and not on the useless apologies of the man sitting on my couch.

"Okay. Sure. You say you don't deserve forgiveness. Is that your way of avoiding apologizing?" My voice sounded light. And disinterested. When, inside, my emotions were anything but.

But I wouldn't give him the satisfaction of seeing me bleed.

"I don't— I didn't, did I?" In a movement too quick for me to avoid, he was up off the couch and kneeling at my feet. "I am so sorry, my baby girl. You're beautiful and smart and strong, and you deserve so much better than me. I'm sorry, whether you can ever forgive me or not."

He reached out as if to take my hands and I flinched away. "Don't do that to me, too. Don't make me see your death. I think you've hurt me enough."

His eyes widened, as if he'd forgotten, which I understood. A lot of people did, once they got to know me. It's just that it was something I could never forget. I could never casually touch a hand or an arm or even a baby. I could never know when the curse, or the gift, or the talent —whatever I chose to call it—would show up and flatten me with knowledge that humans had never been meant to possess.

He stood and moved back to his spot on the couch, where he clasped his hands between his knees and looked down at the floor. "I can't be here long. I just wanted a chance to reach out before... Before I went away. On a trip. I don't know how long I'll be gone, and I don't know where you'll be when I get back, but I just wanted a chance to see you. To tell you I'm so sorry, Tess."

He blew out a long, explosive breath. "I won't bother you again."

And then, before I could even form the words to answer him, he was gone.

Leaving me alone with decades of pain, hundreds of unanswered questions, and one slightly bedraggled stuffed duck.

8

"I was not prepared for the Doltar."

Junior Schwarzendreiven nodded, hitching up his belt again beneath his enormous belly. "Nobody is ever prepared for the Doltar."

After my dad had left the night before, I'd canceled on Molly, sent Jack home, and spent a long night tossing and turning, trying to shut my brain off. At around three in the morning, I gave up and had a Tylenol PM, which at least let me sleep, but nightmares of giant stuffed ducks riding in clown cars chased me around my dreams until I gave up at six, showered, filled up my super-sized travel mug of coffee, and headed into the shop. Then I spent a couple of hours doing paperwork and cleaning—the clown shoe scuff marks were easy to clean up, thankfully—and then opened an hour early at nine, to make up for the afternoon off.

Needless to say, none of this had prepared me for Junior and the Doltar.

I'd known Junior since I was a kid. He was maybe in his mid-eighties, about six feet tall and five feet across, or at least that's how he'd looked to me and Molly when he came into our elementary school to tell us about ventriloquists and put on a show with one of his dummies.

Junior was a bit shrunken these days from how larger-than-life he'd seemed to be to us then. He'd long since retired from doing shows around the country, and he'd become the premiere builder and restorer of ventriloquist dummies in the world.

Yes, we have a lot of people with unusual professions in Dead End.

"What, exactly, is it?" I walked around the machine, which looked like a phone booth with a scary guy wearing a turban inside. Junior had rolled it in on a handcart, and it had barely cleared my door. The cabinet itself must be a few inches over six feet high, and it looked heavy, too.

"Have you heard of the Zoltar machine?"

"Ohhhh. Sure. The fortune-telling machine. I've seen a couple at antique shows Jeremiah and I went to in Atlanta. Is this the dollar store knockoff version?"

He made a face. "Not exactly that. It's very similar to the Zoltar, but the inventor, for whatever reason, made it so it only gives bad-news fortunes. Her girlfriend told her she was a dolt for doing that, or so the story goes, and left her. So the inventor, sad and alone, named the machine the Doltar and tried to sell it. It never really caught on."

"I'm not surprised," I said, examining the gorgeous painted designs on the wooden cabinet. The top half was glass on both sides and the front, so you could look your fill of the creepy upper half of the mannequin, which was dressed in a seriously ugly yellow and green turban and silk pajama outfit. He (Doltar, not Junior) had a handlebar mustache that extended a good six inches from each side of his face.

"Not only is it kind of scary-looking, I bet the Zoltar

company sued them for copyright infringement or stealing their idea or something." I leaned forward to get a closer look and then jumped back, startled, when Doltar lit up like a Christmas tree. His turban glowed, his eyes lit up, and his crystal ball turned purple. Then his arms started moving in a stilted fashion, one waving up and down and the other circling his crystal ball, and his head jerkily moved left and right, as if seeking out a victim.

"That's some battery it must have going on, to do all that."

When Junior didn't answer, I looked up to see that he'd backed all the way across the room to the door. He looked pale and like he was in imminent danger of swallowing his tongue. "I don't—I don't—Tess," he finally managed to get out. "That's just it. Doltar doesn't have batteries. And, as you can see, it's not plugged in."

He pointed to the curl of electric cord tucked in between the cabinet and the cart.

"It must have a backup battery, Mr. Schwarzendreiven," I told him, dropping down to the floor in a crouch to see how to open the bottom panels of the cabinet. "Machines don't just light up and start moving with no power source."

"That's just it," Junior hissed at me, one hand on the door and the other clutching the front of his UCF KNIGHTS FOOTBALL T-shirt. "It doesn't. I think it's ... *possessed.*"

I shot up so fast I hit my head on the slight overhang at the midpoint of the cabinet. "Ouch! It's not possessed, Junior. It has a battery. We just have to figure out how to find it."

His red face drooped. "I thought you of all people would believe me, Tess. Because of your ... your ..."

I knew what he meant, but sometimes I was just not in the mood to help people out when they were, basically, calling me a freak. Instead, I folded my arms and stared at him, daring him to finish that sentence.

Junior had the grace to look sheepish, and he cleared his throat. "Anyway, I'd like to sell it. Will you buy it?"

I sighed. This was my week for unusual items. What I wouldn't give for a few of the normal "take my old TV, please" conversations. Even a lawn mower or two. But ukuleles and Doltars were out of my usual range.

"Let me look it up and see what I can offer you. Would you like some coffee while you wait?"

Doltar, who had calmed down while I was looking for his battery, lit up again. This time, he turned his head toward Junior, opened his animatronic mouth, and spoke. "You will die from a coffee overdose at a young age."

Junior gasped. "Did you hear that? Did you? He foretold my death!"

I rolled my eyes. "Mr. Schwarzendreiven. You are, pardon me for saying it, long past a young age. So it *can't* be about you."

"Maybe—"

"No," I said firmly. "It wasn't even looking at me. It's just a glitch. Let me figure this out."

"I'm going to Mellie's to get donuts. I'll be back later," Junior babbled. "Or, just call me. Yeah, call me. I'll ... later, Tess. I'll see you later."

"But what about your—"

He was out the door before I could finish my sentence. I shook my head and patted the side of the cabinet. "About fifty years off on that one, Doltar. Now calm down and let me figure you out."

Doltar turned his ... *its* ... creepy head to me and opened its mouth. "You will live a life of great oddness."

I laughed. "Oh, Doltar. You have no idea, my friend."

Then I pulled out my laptop and wandered down the rabbit hole of internet research on arcade games.

"Did you know you may be based on a real-life fortune teller from India in the 1920s?"

Doltar didn't answer.

I tried not to feel snubbed.

"This is why pawnshop owners are great at trivia games, by the way," I told him. "And, not for nothing, but you are way easier to talk to than most men."

"Which man are you talking to now?"

I was way too accustomed to Jack's stealthy entrances to let him see me startle these days—it just encouraged him.

I pointed at the Doltar. "The Doltar."

"The what?"

"The Doltar." I told him the history.

"That's kind of weird."

"Weird seems to be my word of the week. Anyway, I like Doltar. He lights up when I talk to him, which is flattering—"

Jack's lazy smile was way too sexy for this early in the morning. "I light up when you talk to me, Tess."

"Only if it's about food. Hey, since you're here, see if you can figure out how to get to its batteries. It's not plugged in, but it still keeps lighting up and doing its thing. It scared poor Mr. Schwarzendreiven so badly that he ran out of here to go get emergency donuts."

Jack paused. "Is he coming back?"

I narrowed my eyes. "See? Food. And you lit right up."

"Okay, okay. I'm looking. Hey, Doltar, where are your batteries?"

The Doltar lit up again and swiveled its head to look at Jack. Instead of talking, though, this time a card slid out of a slot next to the slot for depositing money.

"What does it say?"

Jack shot me a look. "I'm not reading it."

"Chicken!"

"Hey. It's a fortune from a creepy looking mutant fortune teller. I've had enough oddness in my life already without that."

"Fine." I rounded the counter and marched over to Doltar. "If you're afraid to read it, I will. The cooler the cards and fortunes are, the more money I can get for it. People love that stuff."

I reached for the card, which promptly slid back into the machine before I could grab it.

"Not yours," Doltar intoned.

"Okay," I admitted. "That's a little creepy."

Jack gave Doltar his fiercest rebel-leader scowl.

Doltar was unmoved.

In fact, I almost thought I could see his ridiculous mustache quiver with amusement, but that was probably insomnia-induced psychosis.

"Jack?"

Jack sighed. "Fine. Doltar, give me a fortune."

Doltar lit up again, and another card, or maybe the same one, slid out of the slot. This time Jack snatched it before it could disappear again.

"What does it say?"

Jack laughed. "It says BEWARE THE POULTRY."

I blinked. "What in the heck could that mean?"

Then I whirled around to stare at my door. I'd had an unfortunate incident with a live goat a while back, so it was not out of the realm of possibility that someone could show up with a flock of chickens.

In a shocking development, not a single chicken walked in the door.

"Well. That's odd, all right. You should make a fortune on this thing," Jack told me, clearly fighting a grin. "And I promise to help you fight off any feral chickens who invade the shop."

"Whatever. I'm going to go make some more coffee. Want some?"

"No. I'm going to grab my tool bag out of the truck and see if I can find that battery pack for you."

For a moment, I felt guilty that Jack helped me out so much when he had a business—and a life—of his own. But then I put that aside. That's what friends do, and I'd do the same for him.

Well, maybe not the feral chickens.

A girl has to draw the line somewhere.

9

While I waited for the coffee to brew, I finally called my family back. Aunt Ruby picked up on the first ring, shouted for Uncle Mike, and put me on speaker.

I was in serious trouble when they put me on speaker. I retaliated like a real adult and put *them* on speaker, too.

"We were just on our way out the door to come corner you in the shop," she chided. "We know you always hide from emotional turmoil by burying yourself in work."

I gently banged my head against the wall.

Three times.

"I don't—what are you talking about? What emotional turmoil have I hidden from by working?"

"Remember that boy who stole your lunch? You reorganized all the books on our bookshelves by author, genre, and size."

I stared at the phone. "Aunt Ruby. I was ten years old. When does the statute of limitations run out on bringing that up? And he was a jerk! I should have punched him. There were fresh-baked cookies in that lunch!"

Uncle Mike's deep voice came on, and I could tell he was trying not to laugh. "Hey. I would have punched him over cookies. I thought you were very restrained at the time."

"I remember. You took me out for ice cream and then taught me how to throw a left hook out in the barn." I smiled at the memory. Uncle Mike had been my rock, and Aunt Ruby had been my soft place. Caught between them, I'd had a wonderful childhood, and I'd always known how much I was loved.

"You did what?" Aunt Ruby's voice rose. "Mike! A Southern lady does not punch boys over cookies."

"She finds other ways to get even," I said, grinning.

Jack walked into the room. "This is kind of weird. I mean, not rising to Dead End weird, maybe, but, still. There are no batteries in the Doltar."

"The what?" Uncle Mike asked.

"Oh, hey, Mr. Callahan."

"Jack. Don't you have your own job to get to?"

"Uncle Mike! Jack is helping me figure out the Doltar. Try to be nice." I explained about the Doltar.

"Now that I have to see," he said. "I'm on my way over."

"Oh, no, you're not," Aunt Ruby said. "We're going shopping for supplies, since Tess and Jack are coming to dinner tonight, so we can talk about the T-H-O-M-A-S situation."

I closed my eyes and groaned.

"What was that, dear?"

Jack's eyes gleamed with amusement. "I think she said that she actually does know how to spell, ma'am."

"Oh, I know, it's just habit."

"Aunt Ruby. I learned to spell when I was four. When do you think you'll get out of that habit?"

"Well, we have Shelley now."

"Shelley is nine years old—"

"Almost ten! Her birthday is next month. We have to plan a party," Aunt Ruby said. She loved parties.

"Almost ten years old and just won a history fair. I'm betting she knows how to spell, too. When does she get back from science camp? I miss her."

"Sunday. School starts Monday. So, what time will you be here for dinner?"

I sighed. I could never win this kind of conversation. I should know better. "What time do you want us?"

"You could leave the tiger out of this," Uncle Mike grumbled. "Last time he was here, he ate an entire side of beef. I'm going to have to mortgage the house if he keeps coming to dinner."

Jack grinned and took my coffee mug out of my hands and took a sip. "Why don't I bring steaks, sir? I picked up a couple hundred New York strips a few days ago and kept twenty or so in the fridge to grill this weekend. I found a new marinade—"

"Don't go getting all fancy with your marinades, boy. Tried and true wins all, every day, when it comes to grilling. Let me tell you—"

"Yes, yes, okay," Aunt Ruby interrupted. "We need to get going. Tess, we'll see you as soon as you close the shop. Bring Lou if you want, dear."

"I will." I swallowed the lump that was suddenly blocking my throat. "Will he ... will my father be there?"

"You haven't seen him yet?" Aunt Ruby sounded worried and relieved all at once, somehow.

"He came by last night. It ... didn't go well. I'll tell you about it tonight." I didn't want to talk about my father over speaker phone.

I heard Uncle Mike rumble something quietly to Aunt Ruby, and then she came back on the line. "I think we'll just keep it at the four of us. We need to talk."

"I wish people would quit saying that to me," I muttered.

"What? Don't mumble. It's not polite."

"I said, yes, we'll be there. I'll bring something."

"No need. I've got it covered. Bye, dear."

"See you soon, Tess, honey," Uncle Mike rumbled. "Don't forget those steaks, Shepherd."

"Yes, sir," Jack said, handing me back my coffee mug, half empty. "Will do."

I hung up and sighed. "How do they always manipulate me into doing whatever they want?"

"You love them, and you're very good to them." Jack's green gaze and serious expression pinned me in place. "They're very lucky to have you, Tess."

I shrugged, feeling strangely awkward. "I'm lucky to have them. And I guess we have dinner plans now."

"For two people who still haven't gone on our first date, we have a lot of meals together," he said, taking a step closer and touching my cheek.

I blew a strand of hair out of my suddenly hot face. "Yes, and speaking of that, I thought we'd take lunch to Eleanor and Dave around noon. They're at his house, because she's taking care of Dave and Zane while he recovers."

"You'll close the shop?"

I nodded. "We're not that busy today, and I need to research the Doltar, anyway. You can drive us to the deli. I'll call in an order now. Meatball sub?"

He tilted his head. "Philly cheesesteak this time, I think."

I dialed Lauren's Deli and gave her my order: Meatball sub for me, two teriyaki chicken subs for Eleanor and Dave, and five—I glanced at Jack with a raised eyebrow, and he held up six fingers—six cheesesteaks for Jack. Chips, sodas, cookies, all the extras. She promised to have it ready to go at noon, and I shooed Jack over to his office to check his mail and voicemail for any potential clients. His budding P.I. business hadn't been doing very much actual ... business, but, as he'd just demonstrated with the clowns, he didn't exactly need money. The Atlanteans had basically forced him to take a reward for helping save their city, their citizens, and even their royals, more times that he'd admit.

(I confess, I'd researched Atlantis after I'd learned that Jack had been involved with them.)

While he did whatever he did in his office, I got to work. I had paperwork to do, payroll data to get to my bookkeeper (yes, I paid Eleanor for the hours she would have worked when Dave got shot, so sue me, I'm a softy), and, always, tidying up the inventory. I hoped some customers came in, too, so I could pay the bills.

"And you can watch out for the deadly chickens, okay, Doltar?"

Doltar had nothing to say to that.

~

At noon, Jack wandered out of his office with an oddly contemplative expression on his face.

"What's up? The feral chickens show up on your side of the building?"

He grinned, but it was half-hearted. "No, strangely enough. I have a case."

"Really? What? Who?"

"I can't actually talk about it, yet," he said slowly.

I was a little bit disappointed, since I told him everything, but I realized his business held a lot more confidentiality issues than mine did, so I just shrugged.

"Okay. Well, good luck, I guess. Let's head out to get that lunch."

Lauren's Deli was packed, as usual, with a line out the door of people waiting to pick up their lunch. I kept telling her she should put in some tables for people who wanted to eat in, but she always said people were slobs, and they could take their food to go, so she didn't have to clean up after them.

I had no good argument for that.

Jack waited in the truck, making a call, while I went in. Larry from Dead End Towing was in line in front of me, so we chatted a bit, and he told me he hadn't seen any new crashes out on the stretch of road where an enormous alligator sent by a witch had attacked me, causing me to run my old car into a tree. Shelley's parents had died on that road, too, so I was glad that the danger had disappeared with the death of the black magic witch who'd caused it all.

When I got up to the counter, Lauren looked at me, looked at the two large bags that contained my order, and shook her head sadly. "Tess. We really need to talk about this eating problem you're developing."

I laughed. "It's more of a tiger problem, really."

"Yeah, I saw that the hot tiger is out in the truck. Are you two an item? Just ..." her cheeks turned pink. "Asking for a friend."

"We ... yeah. We kind of are," I said, handing her my credit card and feeling my face get hot, too. "He's, I mean, I, um ..."

"No worries. I get it." She ran my card and handed me my receipt. "If he has any brothers, though, send them my way, okay?"

"Will do," I promised, grabbing my bags and trying to

ignore all the knowing grins of everyone who'd been in line behind me as I rushed out.

Back at the truck, I put the bags in the back seat and then climbed in the front. "Well. If you ever want to date someone who actually makes food all the time, Lauren is interested."

He glanced at me and grinned. "I hope you told her I only have eyes for you."

I rolled my eyes and said nothing, but I caught myself smiling all the way to Dave's house.

Dave had bought a hundred-year-old home on the outskirts of town and turned it into a showpiece. He said that if anybody wanted to hire his construction company, all they had to do was drive by his house to see that he did good work.

And that was definitely the truth. It was a beautiful old Victorian, complete with a tower, a turret, and a porch that wrapped around the entire house. It was a true Painted Lady, in shades of blue, peach, and white, and it was the most beautiful house in town (after mine), in my opinion. Eleanor loved to garden, so the landscaping was as lovely as the house, and the porch was decorated with pots of gorgeous, colorful flowers.

When we pulled up outside, Jack jumped out of the truck, grabbed the food, and bounded up the stairs to the beautiful wood-and-glass door, where he ignored the doorbell and pounded on the door instead.

"Lunch delivery for Dave! We brought *extra buns!*"

I groaned. "Really? How long have you been practicing that one?"

"Since I found out he was okay, pretty much." He turned and grinned at me, and the sun struck his head just enough to bring out the deep red and bright gold highlights in the bronze of his hair.

I had to remind myself to breathe.

It was one thing to agree to go out with him and banter about it, but when I actually remembered how unbelievably hot he was ... I kind of felt out of my league.

Let's be honest, I really didn't even have a league.

Owen the dentist had been my league, except not really.

I sighed, feeling sad, and Jack leaned over and kissed the top of my head.

"Come on. It can't have been worse than the cannibals and the clown joke."

Dave threw open the door before I could answer, and fake-glared at Jack. "Extra buns? Really? Your best friend has been *shot*—"

"In the ass," Jack interjected.

"*Shot*, and you come here to mock me?"

Jack shoved a bag of food at him. "I came here to bring you lunch. The mocking is just a bonus."

"David, you invite our guests inside," Eleanor called out. "And you two behave, or Tess and I will eat all the sandwiches."

We trooped inside and crossed beautifully finished hardwood floors to the open, bright kitchen.

"Nice threat, Eleanor, except there's no way we could eat all of this food," I said, depositing my bag on the white quartz countertop. "Let's just feed them and hope they stop talking long enough to eat."

Jack pulled out a chair at the enormous farmhouse table. "Why don't you have a *seat*, Dave?"

Dave groaned. "I'm in serious pain, here, and you're making it worse."

"Oh, no!" I rushed over to him. "Jack, leave him alone. Dave, can I get you anything?"

Dave smiled at me and gave me a one-armed hug. "You, I like. You can stay. Make your furry friend go chase a mouse or something."

Eleanor bustled over with plates and cups. "Now, you stop teasing that girl. You told me it barely hurts, with the pain meds they gave you."

I sighed but didn't bother to point out that 'that girl' was her boss. Some things would never change.

The food smelled so good, we all dove in, and there wasn't talking for a while. When three of us were nibbling at cookies, and Jack was down to his fifth sandwich, Dave finally spoke up about what had happened.

"It was completely out of the blue. This guy walked into my office and told me his boss was going to be my new partner." Dave shook his head, his eyes shadowed at the memory. "I was so taken aback I thought he was joking, and I laughed."

Jack put his sandwich down. "Mobsters don't generally like being laughed at," he said, his words falling like bricks, hard and sharp-edged. "Then what happened?"

"Then I told him I wasn't taking on any partners, and he pulled out a gun, and shit got real serious, real fast."

Eleanor made a small noise of distress, and I patted her arm.

"He's okay now, Eleanor."

"I know, but it could have been so much worse. You can bet I'll be in the front row in church on Sunday." She blinked rapidly, fighting back the tears.

"Then what did he say?" Jack leaned forward, the rest of his food forgotten. "Did he name any names? What did he look like?"

Dave's lips thinned. "I don't want you going after them. They're dangerous."

"*I'm* dangerous, Dave. They're just thugs."

"It's too late, anyway," I told him. "We think they're the ones who confronted us in Beau's. So, we're already on their radar. You may as well give us as much information as you have."

Dave stared at me for a long moment, then nodded. "That makes sense, I guess. I told Susan all of it."

He described the man who'd shot him, and Jack and I looked at each other.

"You won't have to worry about him anymore," Jack said. "He came out the loser in a man-meets-truck incident at Beau's."

"That was him? The dairy truck?" Eleanor raised her hand to her throat. "Oh, my goodness. Rooster Jenkins' nephew was driving that truck, and he was really upset, I hear. The man just backed out into the road in front of him, almost like somebody pushed him."

I pointed at Jack. "You didn't tell me that."

He shrugged. "I didn't see it clearly enough to be sure, but I had my suspicions. I just didn't know why, and you didn't need to hear about more violence."

"Don't ever again decide what I do and don't need to hear," I said evenly. "I am not a child, and that man died after I saw a vision about it. You had no right to withhold the truth from me."

It took him a moment, but he finally nodded. "You're right. I'm sorry. It won't happen again."

Dave started clapping. "Now that's a beautiful thing. Jack Shepherd apologizing. This is the kind of situation I can really get *behind.*"

Jack threw his head back and laughed, and I just

groaned. Again. "Seriously? You're telling butt jokes on yourself?"

"Hey, once a ten-year-old boy, always a ten-year-old boy," Dave said, grinning. "Want to hear some fart jokes?"

I stood, clearing away my trash. "Okay, that's my cue. I need to get back to work."

Eleanor stood, too. "Don't worry about that, Tess, I've got it. Thanks so much for lunch. I'll try to come into work tomorrow, but—"

"No, you won't. Stay here and take care of your boys—where is Zane, by the way? Which camp? I know you told me."

"He's at science camp with Shelley. They're having a great time together."

I smiled to hear about Shelley making a friend. "They'll be in the same class at school, right? Or is she behind because of missing so much school when everything happened?"

"Oh, no. They wouldn't keep her back. She's so smart, Tess."

I grinned. "Well, she *is* my sister."

Eleanor hugged me. "Thanks for everything. I'll be in Monday for my regular hours, if nothing else horrible happens."

Jack patted her arm. "I'm going to make sure nothing else horrible ever happens to Dave again, Eleanor. I'll catch the *bums* who were behind this, that's a promise."

This time, everybody groaned.

Dave punched Jack in the shoulder, which seems to be "guy" for "I love you, too, bro," and we started out the door. When we were going down the porch stairs to the truck, though, Dave called out and stopped us.

"Hey. I think I kind of blanked this out before, but you

should know it. When that thug was in my office, he picked out a photo of me and Tess with Zane at the beach from last summer, and, well, it was strange." Dave's face turned serious. "He asked me how I knew Tess."

I felt my knees go kind of funny, but I grabbed the railing. Jack's muscles tensed and he leaned forward on the balls of his feet. "What did you say?"

"I didn't say anything. I was too busy jumping out the window after I saw the gun. The rest you know."

"Thanks, Dave," I said, smiling as best as I could. "I appreciate the heads-up."

"Damn," Jack said, grinning at Dave. "If only I could have worked *bottoms up* into a sentence. A missed opportunity if ever there was one."

We waved goodbye, and I didn't say another word until we were in the truck. "Why do they want to know about me?"

Jack's face had gone hard and dangerous. "I don't know, but I intend to find out."

"You don't think they know about my pawnshop, do you?"

"Let's assume they know everything. Do me a favor. Call Lucky."

He handed me his phone, and I pulled up Lucky's number. I may be a fairly brave person, and I was getting to be a better shot, but if mobsters had taken a personal interest in me, I had no disagreement at all with having one or more of our ex-Special Forces friends come hang out at the shop for a while, until we sorted this out.

"Maybe they left town after their guy died," I said, hopefully.

"Have we ever had that kind of luck?"

I made the call.

When we got back to the shop, there were three black SUVs lined up in front.

Jack stopped the truck and started to turn around, but I put a hand on his arm. "We may as well find out what they want. It's not like they're going to go away if we avoid them."

O'Sullivan stepped out of the backseat of one of them and waved to us. "I just want to talk," he called out.

"I don't trust him," Jack growled.

"I don't either, but here we are. Let's ask him what this is about. I'm calling 911 now, so Susan or somebody will be on the way." I started dialing.

When Belle, the dispatcher who'd worked at the sheriff's office since dinosaurs walked the earth, came on the line, I quickly filled her in, and she promised she'd send someone out immediately. She was a terrible gossip, and not my favorite person, but she was efficient and did her job well, so I thanked her and hung up.

Then I set my phone to RECORD, and Jack and I got out of the truck.

"What do you want, O'Sullivan? Seems like you should be running off home after your man got hit by that truck," Jack said.

I held my phone, screen down, against my leg and said nothing.

O'Sullivan looked at me. "I have a proposition for you."

"I'm not interested." I looked in his eyes and saw nothing but emptiness, and a shiver swept through me, but I stood my ground. "I'm ... I'm sorry about your friend."

He laughed, and it was an ugly, bitter sound like cut glass on stone. "He wasn't my friend. He just worked for me. And you told him he'd live a long, happy life, so I tested your prediction by pushing him into the road. Hit by a truck isn't a long, happy life. I wanted to see how good your visions actually are."

"I lied," I said quietly. "But I did warn him."

"Yeah. O'Brien told me. Just after the truck hit Smitty." He eyed me with a dark intensity. "So, now we want to work with you."

"Not a chance," Jack snarled, stepping partially in front of me.

"I don't have any intention of working with you, in any capacity," I told O'Sullivan, moving back up to stand next to Jack. "Please just go away."

"Remember, when this turns ugly, that I asked nicely," O'Sullivan said. Three of his men stepped out of the SUVs as if by signal.

Jack shook his head. "Big mistake, O'Sullivan. Huge."

"Why are you even here?" I could hear the faint sound of sirens, which meant that Jack had surely already heard them, and I wanted to distract and delay them until Susan got here.

"I'm collecting what's mine, Tess Callahan, and you're

just a bonus. Although, I know the Irish always stick together, so if you know Thomas O'Malley, you'd be doing yourself a favor if you tell me where he is."

"The *Aristocats*?" I blurted out.

"What?" He and Jack both looked at me.

"Thomas O'Malley. It's ... never mind. No, I don't know any Thomas O'Malley."

His icy gaze searched my face, but I'm pretty transparent and a terrible liar, so he realized pretty quickly I was telling the truth, I guessed. And, anyway, the sirens were really loud and really close now.

"We'll be in touch, Miss Callahan," O'Sullivan said, turning to leave.

"No. You won't," Jack told him. Then, still in human form, he leapt into the air, shifting mid-leap and landing on the roof of O'Sullivan's SUV in tiger form.

And then he roared.

Two of O'Sullivan's thugs screamed and dove for the ground. The other one turned and started running.

There's not much scarier than a full-grown Bengal tiger in full fury.

O'Sullivan, though, was made of tougher fiber. He took an involuntary step back, but then he stood his ground.

"You don't want to head down this path with me, Shepherd," he said.

Jack deliberately took one huge paw, extended his claws, and ripped the metal off the roof of the car like it was butter.

That's when the sheriff's car peeled around the corner, with Deputy Kelly at the wheel.

Deputy Andrew Kelly was a slender, rather short man who was my age or so but looked like he was just entering puberty. He had red hair, freckles, and a shy smile, and he could be a real badass when he needed to be. He slammed the car into park, jumped out of the car, and aimed his gun.

At O'Sullivan.

"I know for sure that if Jack is this enraged, you have done something very, very wrong, Mister," Andy said.

Jack's tongue flopped out the side of his mouth in a big tiger smile, and then he jumped off the SUV and stalked over to my side, where he shifted back to human.

"Hey, Deputy," Jack said. "Nice to see you. Mr. O'Sullivan here was just threatening Tess."

The two thugs on the ground hurriedly pushed themselves up, brushed themselves off, and climbed in the SUV. The third one was long gone, maybe in the next county by now.

"I don't want to press any charges," I said. "I just want them to leave and never come back."

O'Sullivan's dead gaze brushed me and then turned to Andy, who holstered his gun.

"There are no grounds for charges, Officer. We were just having a friendly conversation."

"Right. I heard about your friendly conversation in town," Andy said. "You need to leave, now. If I hear about you bothering Tess again, I'll throw you in jail."

"Your mayor may have something to say about that," O'Sullivan said silkily.

Andy laughed. "You are in the wrong place, sir, if you think that corrupt city officials hold any sway over duly appointed officers of the law. Dead End is far different from wherever you come from—"

"It's different than from where *anybody* comes from," Jack put in.

"—and we don't put up with people threatening our citizens. Now, get back in your car and get out of my town."

If looks could actually kill, all three of us would be dead right there in my parking lot, from the scowl O'Sullivan was blazing at us.

I shrugged. I'd seen worse.

"As you say, Deputy." He climbed in his car, and the SUVs pulled out in a sedate line. O'Sullivan stared at me all the way out of the parking lot.

"What does he want with you, Tess?" Deputy Kelly gave me a concerned look, which made me smile. He was so sweet.

"I honestly don't know. I think he's fascinated with my ... ability."

"Oh. I heard about Beau's. I'm sorry that happened to you."

"Me, too, Andy. Thanks. If you don't need me, I'm going to get back to work. I need a nice, ordinary afternoon."

"Sure. I'll talk to Jack about anything I need to know."

I tossed him a smile and headed for my shop, the soundtrack to *The Aristocats* suddenly running through my brain.

By the time Jack finished filling Andy in and walked in the door, ten or so minutes later, I'd figured it out.

"*The Aristocats* was my favorite movie when I was a toddler. I watched it over and over and over and had all the songs memorized."

Jack blinked. "Okay. Is there a reason I need to know this?"

"It was a Disney movie. About a pampered French cat named Duchess and her kittens. The evil butler ... well, never mind him. Duchess fell in love with an alley cat."

He grinned. "Is this a metaphor for you and me? Alley cat, huh? I've been called worse, Duchess."

I grabbed his arms. "The alley cat. He was named *Thomas O'Malley*."

Jack's puzzled expression told me he still didn't get it.

"Jack. I watched that movie over and over from the time I was a baby, practically. One of my only memories of my parents is them watching it with me, and my dad singing the song."

"What song?" But I could see the dawning realization in his eyes.

"There were other names, too, but the important ones in the song were this: *I'm Thomas O'Malley, O'Malley, the alley cat.*"

Jack swore beneath his breath. "Thomas O'Malley—"

"Is my father."

~

*A*fter that, I spent the afternoon doing absolutely ordinary things, which of course felt odd under the circumstances. I didn't have my father's phone number, and my big realization wasn't something I wanted to tell Aunt Ruby and Uncle Mike over the phone. Instead, I was left to ponder why he'd taken an alias from something that meant so much to me and used it to, apparently, do very bad things.

Or at least I assumed they were bad. He was mixed up with the mob somehow, that much was clear. I kept coming back to how he'd said he sure didn't need any money. Had he stolen money from O'Sullivan? I didn't know much about mobsters, but that seemed like a really stupid move to me.

I needed to talk to Mike and Ruby. I needed to put all this out of my mind and get to work. The bells over my door chimed, and a group of women walked in, chatting and laughing, and I put on my business face and got to work.

Jack kept the connecting door between us open and periodically popped his head in, but he was on nonstop phone calls all afternoon, reaching out to his contacts to see what he could learn about O'Sullivan. No matter what else he might be, the man was human, so Jack's supernatural contacts didn't seem to know much about him. At around three in the afternoon, though, Jack looked in and gave me a thumbs up, while still on the phone, so I figured he'd learned something and he 'd tell me about it on the way to dinner.

I'd sold a couple hundred dollars' worth of items to the women, who'd taken selfies with the **WE DO NOT DEAL IN VAMPIRE TEETH, EVER** sign, giggling in that way that only people who've never met a real, live (dead?) vampire can giggle. A few minutes after they'd left, my door opened again, and this time a familiar figure stood there grinning at me.

"Otis!" I walked over to shake his hand. It was nice to see him again. "It's been a while. What have you been up to?"

Otis was an indeterminate age, worn, lean, and wiry, and a proud redneck through and through, as his shirt proclaimed. I'd known him for years.

Otis glanced up at Fluffy, our shop mascot. He'd pawned it with first Jeremiah and then me, over and over and over, until I finally just offered him money to buy it. He'd been friends with Fluffy when she was alive, and then kept her after she died. It had been a strange and beautiful relationship, but now he evidently had made another friend.

I bent down to say hello to the beautiful greyhound at his side. "Well, how are you, beautiful girl?"

The dog studied me with calm brown eyes and then nudged my hand with her nose. I obliged with pets and ear scratches.

"Who's this, Otis?"

"This is Beauty. Well, her real name is ..." He pulled a

crumpled piece of paper out of his baggy khaki pants. "Anderson's Champion Sleeping Beauty of Provence," he finished, his chest puffed out. "She's a real champion racing greyhound."

I frowned and stood. "I'm sorry, but I'm not a fan of racing dogs, as you know. In fact, not a fan is a vast under-statement. I worked on the campaign to get it banned."

"I know, Tess. She's one of the retired dogs that the grey-hound rescue adopted out after the tracks closed." He smiled down at Beauty. " I adopted her."

From the way Otis had cared for Fluffy, in her life and beyond, I knew Beauty was going to have a very good life.

"She's very lucky to have you, then," I said, and Otis rewarded me with a huge, slightly gap-toothed smile.

"Oh!" I walked back to the jewelry counter. "I have a present for Beauty."

I unlocked the counter and took out a sterling silver charm in the shape of a dog bone. "Here. This is just big enough to put her name on one side, and your name and phone number on the other side, just in case. You can put it on that lovely pink collar you gave her."

Otis's mouth fell open, and his cheeks turned rosy. "You —that's real nice of you, Tess. I don't—are you sure I can't pay you for it?"

"Nope. It's a gift. To celebrate your beautiful new friend. Beauty is a good name for her. Bring her by to visit any time."

He gave me a bashful smile, but then looked down in surprise at the dog when she stiffened and started to growl. "What is it, girl?"

"Sorry." Jack walked in from his side of the building. "She probably senses me. Let me just say hello."

He calmly walked up to Otis and the dog, both of whom

were trembling, and he crouched down in front of Beauty and looked in her eyes. Within seconds, she calmed down, sat, and held up one paw for him to shake, which he did, before standing and shaking Otis's hand, too.

"Nice to see you, Shepherd," Otis said, squaring his shoulders and looking up at Jack. "How do you like my new dog?"

"She's gorgeous," Jack said. "If she ever wants to go running, give me a call and bring her out to my house."

Otis's face was a study in consternation. "Um, I don't think ... she might ..."

Jack grinned at him. "As me, not as a tiger, Otis. I can run pretty fast on two legs, too, and she might have fun going for a couple of miles with me."

Otis's muscles relaxed. "Oh. Okay. Well, maybe. But she's retired. I think she might like to lie on the couch, watch TV, and eat bacon all day."

I sighed wistfully. "Who wouldn't like that?"

Honestly, it sounded better than my plans for the evening. I loved my aunt and uncle, but I didn't really want to have a heart-to-heart about my father. Or about Thomas O'Malley.

We chatted with Otis for a few more minutes, and then he went off to the Pit Stop, grocery and bait shop, to buy the bacon for the TV marathon he had planned. Beauty glanced back at us and then followed Otis out of my shop, headed for a life in the lap of redneck luxury.

"Good for him," I said. "That dog is going to have a wonderful life."

Jack nodded. "Bacon and TV sounded pretty good to me, too."

"What did you find out?"

We got bottles of water, and then Jack filled me in.

"Mostly, nothing. People had heard of him but didn't know much about him, or didn't think much of him. But then I finally got lucky with a contact in the NYC shifter community."

"Shifters?"

"Cat shifters. Lynx, panther, some others. Anyway, he said the rumor is that somebody stole a lot of money from O'Sullivan, who left town to go after it. And—maybe—something much worse."

I gulped water and tried not to think about what would be worse than stealing a lot of money from a mobster, but finally I had to ask. "How much worse?"

"My contact says the thief also got away with files on O'Sullivan's planned expansion. He plans to merge the Irish mob with a wolf shifter pack from upstate New York and take over all organized crime in the Northeast. Whoever got away with the information got everything—times, dates, plans, financials. Everything."

"Oh, no." I suddenly found it hard to breathe. "You think my father is the thief?"

He shrugged, but his expression was somber. "I don't know. What do you think?"

"I think we need to call Alejandro. It's time to get the FBI's Paranormal Operations division in on this."

"I agree, but I wasn't going to call him without asking you first. He's your dad."

"Yes, but he didn't tell us anything," I said, anger growing. "He left me to muddle into this situation with O'Sullivan ignorant of what might be going on. If he's really the one who stole this information, maybe Alejandro knows what we can do and how we can get the mob out of Dead End."

"And surely he'll know people in the non-paranormal

side of things who have an idea of what to do about O'Sullivan, either way."

I nodded and pulled my phone out of my pocket. "I'll play him the recording I took of our conversation with O'Sullivan in the parking lot, too."

Jack raised an eyebrow. "Tess, not that it matters on this, but it's illegal to secretly record someone in Florida."

"Not in Black Cypress County. You know we have our own charter. We don't have to play by state or federal rules. Maybe it's time Mr. O'Sullivan finds that out."

11

After closing the shop, we picked up Lou at my place, the steaks at Jack's place, and headed to the house where I grew up. Aunt Ruby and Uncle Mike lived in a beautifully maintained old farmhouse about five miles from my house, and kept chickens, goats, and a very old horse on the property. They were the only family I'd really known, and they were the best family any girl who'd lost both parents could have asked for.

Or any girl at all.

I smiled when I saw Uncle Mike sitting out on the front porch swing, pretending not to be waiting for us.

"We spent a lot of time out on that swing when I was a kid. He'd talk me down from school problems, boy problems, and anything else that made me cry."

Jack glanced at me, smiling a little. "Am I a boy problem?"

I refused to answer on general principles.

Uncle Mike stood, just so he could look down at Jack, I suspected, and waved at me to hurry up. "Let's get those steaks going, I'm not getting any younger."

I kissed his cheek and handed over Lou, who adored him and promptly went boneless in his arms and started purring like a motorboat. "You're not getting any older, either."

My uncle was a retired engineer who was good at everything, up to and including keeping the peace in a home with two stubborn females. He was tall and lean, had brilliantly white hair, and had lost one of the true joys of his life when I replaced my wrecked Toyota with a Mustang, so he couldn't criticize my foreign-made car anymore.

"How's the new car holding up? Changing the oil regularly?"

"I haven't even had it for five thousand miles yet, okay? I'm paying attention, don't worry."

Uncle Mike eyed Jack. "Shepherd."

"Sir."

"Is that enough meat for all of us?"

I grabbed his arm. "Please. He probably brought twenty pounds of meat. You know him."

"I know he eats me out of house and home," Uncle Mike grumbled.

Jack grinned. "I can always start telling you stories about antique dental equipment, like her ex did."

Uncle Mike shuddered. I threw up my hands and headed into the house and away from both of them. "At least Owen was a nice person," I yelled back at them.

"Is that you?" Ruby came hurrying out from the kitchen and threw her arms around me, like she hadn't seen me in years. "Oh, my baby. My poor baby."

Oh, boy.

I should have brought a bottle of wine for this.

She burst into tears and grabbed for a tissue from her apron pocket, and I patted her arm. "It's okay, Aunt Ruby. It really is. I didn't expect anything from him, not after all this time. You know that you and Uncle Mike are my family. He's just ... a bad memory."

He wasn't, though. Not entirely. The memory of him singing the songs from my favorite movie was still too fresh in my mind for that to be true. But I put that aside for now.

"What can I do? I'm starving! And it smells great in here."

"It really does, ma'am," Jack said, following us down the hall. "As always. You are the best cook I've even met, and that's the absolute truth."

"You're not getting extra pie, so just cut it out," Uncle Mike grumbled under his breath. "She can see right through you and your flattery."

"It's true," Jack protested.

Aunt Ruby, who hadn't heard the interplay, since she'd hurried ahead to check something in the oven, turned to beam at Jack. "And I made an extra pie just for you, young man."

Jack flashed his biggest smile at her. "You are amazing. Thank you so much."

When she turned back to the stove, he grinned at Uncle Mike. "You were saying?"

"Tiger. Skin. Rug," my uncle said, enunciating very clearly. "Right in the living room, next to my reading chair."

Jack threw back his head and laughed, and a shiver of anticipation tingled down my spine. This wonderful guy, who fit in so well with my family, liked me. Wanted to go out with me. Said I was special.

Somehow, that made all the rest of the crap going on in my life this week just a little bit easier to bear.

"All right, let's not stand around here blathering, let's get that meat on the grill." Uncle Mike led Jack out to the back porch, and Aunt Ruby grabbed my arm and pulled me to sit next to her at the kitchen table.

"Tell me all about it, honey. He was here, and all he wanted to do was see you, but he was worried you wouldn't want to see him. We talked him into waiting to meet you here tonight, for dinner, but then I guess he went to the shop?"

I nodded. "Yes, and then he showed up at my house. We ... talked. I guess. A little. He didn't have much to say. He finally apologized, but I feel like I pushed him into it. Mostly, it made me sad."

She shook her head. "What kind of person stays away from his own daughter for all those years?"

I sighed. "This seems to be my year for finding long-lost relatives. First my grandmother and now Thomas—well. At least Leona wasn't in the mob."

"She was caught up in those banshee murders, though, and ..Oh, my word! Did you say the mob? Is Thomas a ... a ... criminal?" Her face turned so pale it almost matched her "my hairdresser calls this shade Southern blonde" hair.

I had not meant to let that slip. Dang.

I leaned in and hugged her again, content to breathe in her wonderful scent of vanilla and spice. "We're not sure, to be honest. But there are some bad men in town who seem to know him. Maybe. It's all very confusing. Why don't we get dinner on the table, eat, and then we can talk this all out with Uncle Mike and Jack, so I don't have to tell it twice?"

She agreed, but she wasn't happy about it. It seemed wrong to see such a worried expression on her face, so I nudged her to talk to me about Shelley, and how camp was going, and whether she was ready to go through elementary school all over again.

"Don't think we won't be calling on you, young lady." She

waved a serving spoon at me. "You're much closer to understanding this new math than we are."

I laughed. "I bet Uncle Mike has forgotten more math than I ever learned. I just needed to know enough to run a business, not design time machines."

"Farm equipment, dear. What would we do with a time machine? Here, put the beans on the table, and I'll get the potatoes and the pasta salad."

Jack and Uncle Mike walked back in with a tray of grilled steaks, and we all got settled and dug into a really excellent dinner. I know it's not very sophisticated for a twenty-six-year-old woman to spend Friday night with her family, instead of out clubbing or partying or whatever, but it suited me just fine. Especially after how vulnerable seeing my dad had made me feel.

Jack ate his first three steaks before coming up for air, and Uncle Mike put down his steak knife and stared at him. "Where do you put it? I swear, you must have an extra stomach somewhere."

"He does weigh around five hundred pounds in his other form," I reminded my uncle. "Not that I understand, still, where the extra ... *Jack* ... goes when he's not a tiger."

Jack stabbed a fourth steak off the platter. "Pass the rolls, please?"

Aunt Ruby handed him the bread basket. "You ignore them and eat as much as you like, Jack. You're a growing boy."

Uncle Mike snatched a roll before Jack could take the last two. "Boy grows any bigger, and we'll have to buy a bigger house."

"Speaking of houses, what do you think about the roof on Jeremiah's place? I'm thinking I need to have it redone,"

Jack said, which got Uncle Mike off the subject of Jack's appetite and onto home repair, one of his favorites.

Discussion of roof tiles and new windows got us through the rest of dinner, but by the time Aunt Ruby brought out the pies (apple, peach, and blueberry) and the ice cream, the conversation had slowed. Everyone was dancing around the elephant—father—in the room, so I figured it was time to bring him up.

"Do you know where he is?"

Uncle Mike shook his head. "No. He gave me a phone number, but it just rings and rings and doesn't go to a voice-mail or anything. He told us that he was in trouble, and he needed to get out of the country for awhile, but he wanted to say goodbye to Tess first."

He frowned and reached over and patted my hand. "I'm sorry, honey. I know this hasn't been easy on you. If it helps, you don't have any other missing relatives that we know about."

"A few cousins on my mother's side," Aunt Ruby said, looking thoughtful. "But we never associated with that side of the family, so they probably won't show up now."

I put my head down on my arms on the table and started laughing. What else could I do? Cry? I was tougher than that.

Jack smoothed my hair away from my face, and when I looked up at him, his expression was completely unguarded for once. A rarity for him. And what I saw made my breath catch in my throat. It was ... caring.

He really cared about me, and the emotion blazed in his beautiful green eyes for a long moment before he caught himself and blinked, his face reassuming its normal calm expression.

But it was too late. I'd seen it.

Now I just needed to know how to feel about it.

Part of me wanted to jump into his arms, but part of me wanted to run away. Jack scared me—no. It wasn't that Jack scared me. It was that the idea of what we might be together scared me.

And now wasn't the time to think of any of it.

I sat up and shook my hair out of my face

Uncle Mike pointed at Jack. "Touch that pie, and you die."

Jack froze, spatula hovering over the last slice of blueberry pie.

"You already ate half of it, and I only had once piece," my uncle said. "Hand it over."

Jack made puppy-dog eyes at Aunt Ruby. "But tigers love blueberries."

She wagged a finger at Uncle Mike. "You don't need another piece of pie. Remember what the doctor said about your cholesterol. Let Jack have that one."

He snatched the pie pan right out from under Jack's spatula. "Over my dead body."

Jack leaned in and grinned, showing a lot of teeth. "That can be arranged."

Uncle Mike looked at me. "Did I mention I bought new shells for the shotgun?"

I rolled my eyes. "You two need to behave, or I'll—"

Jack suddenly shot up out of his chair so fast that it crashed into the wall behind him.

Uncle Mike looked at him, looked down at the pie, and then back at Jack. "Well, if you feel that strongly about it—"

"Somebody's on your porch," Jack snapped. "And it didn't sound friendly. Stay here."

Naturally, we all followed him. Uncle Mike stopped to grab his shotgun out of the spare room on the way. Jack pointed at me and made a 'stay back' motion that I obeyed instantly, pulling Aunt Ruby with me. Neither she nor I had been soldiers, and I was smart enough to know when I was out of my element.

I was a pawnshop owner, not a fighter.

Uncle Mike took up position on the other side of the door, shotgun at the ready, and nodded at Jack. Jack flung the door open and then snarled something under his breath that sounded like he was swearing in a language I'd never heard.

"Tess. It's your father. Get him in the house and call the sheriff and maybe an ambulance. I'm going to look for whoever did this to him." With that, he shoved open the screen door, leapt over the huddled, bloody heap that was my father and all the way off the porch. By the time I got to the door, he was nothing but an orange, white, and black-striped blur racing off into the distance.

I fell to my knees on the porch and touched my father's sleeve with a shaking hand. He was so badly beaten that I couldn't even tell if he was alive or dead. I could hear Aunt Ruby on the phone to get the deputy and an ambulance, and I saw Uncle Mike put himself and the shotgun between us and anyone who might be lurking behind the trees or out by the barn.

But I didn't care about any of it. I only knew that I might have lost my father before I even got a chance to know him.

"Daddy?"

He opened his eyes.

12

The sheriff came out, and he refused to speak to her.

The ambulance came out, and he refused to let them take him.

My father—my stubborn, wounded father—refused to go anywhere or do anything but lie on the couch, holding tight to my arm. Even as injured as he was, though, he was careful not to touch my bare skin, and I was thankful for that. Knowing what I knew now, I especially had no desire to see how he'd die.

Susan pulled Jack aside and they talked, glancing over at me, but I ignored them, and then she left. The EMTs talked to Aunt Ruby and left some pain meds, after they'd cleaned up the worst of the injuries, but they were very unhappy that he wouldn't go with them.

The one in charge, a curvy woman with high cheekbones, red lipstick, and deep brown skin, told the tall, pale guy who worked with her to take the stuff out to the rig, and then she stopped and looked at me.

"If he starts to convulse, he needs to go to the hospital. If he loses consciousness, he needs to go to the hospital. If he spikes a high fever—"

"He needs to go to the hospital. Got it," I answered.

She pursed her lips. "No, clearly you don't get it, or you'd be encouraging him to come with us."

I squared my shoulders. "Under normal circumstances, I would. But whoever did this to him might be coming back, and I can't protect him—or any innocent bystanders—in the hospital."

"We have security," she shot back.

I pointed at Jack and Uncle Mike. "I have them."

She'd seen Jack shift from tiger back to man, and she took a long look at them both, then finally nodded. "Noted. Just give him fluids, get him to rest, and I hope for all your sakes that this kind of trouble doesn't come looking for him again."

"From your mouth to God's ear," Aunt Ruby said, rubbing her hands up and down her arms and shivering.

Uncle Mike noticed and put his arm around her and led her down to the kitchen to make tea, murmuring to her as they went. I hated that my father had brought his trouble here, to them, but there was no way I was letting him go back out into the night, unprotected.

"What happened? Did O'Sullivan do this to you?"

He closed his eyes and turned his face away.

"You're going to have to tell me, one way or another. You brought this to us, and now we have to deal with it."

His eyes snapped open. "No, you don't. That's why I was leaving. So none of this ever touched you. I just wanted a chance to say goodbye, in case—"

"In case this happened?" Jack walked over and stared down at him, and there was no pity in his expression. "In case he killed you?"

"Maybe I deserve it," Thomas muttered.

"But does Tess? You know he's after her, right?"

My father came up off the couch, in spite of how much it must hurt, rising to a sitting position. "What are you talking about?"

"Oh, so *that* got your attention, *Thomas O'Malley*." Jack's voice dripped scorn. "Didn't it occur to you that a man as careful and thorough as O'Sullivan would research a place before he followed you to it? And what's the most interesting thing a news search would turn up about Dead End? Tess Callahan, Oracle of Death."

I inhaled sharply, and Jack winced.

"Don't ever call me that again."

"I didn't. Or, rather, it's just one of the things the press called you back when that first incident occurred," he said, regret darkening his eyes. "Tess, no matter how much they want your father, you are almost as interesting. *You can tell them how someone will die.* Just imagine how useful the average scum-sucking mob boss would find that talent to be."

My father's eyes darted around the room, as if looking for an escape. His face was swollen and bruised, and one eye was trying to swell shut. His lips were split, and bruises ringed his throat.

Those were just the bruises I could see. Based on how he moved, they'd hurt him just as badly elsewhere. Maybe broken ribs, the EMT had said.

And he'd refused treatment.

Why?

"Why didn't you want to go to the hospital?"

He sighed and moved a little bit, wincing. "You were right. I'm safer outside of the hospital. Sully has killed more people in hospitals than most diseases. And it's not like the

Orlando hospital system is prepared for what a man like him can bring to rain down on them. New York, maybe, but he still gets to them there—his enemies. Here? I'd be dead within the hour."

Jack sat down and pulled me up off the floor, where I was kneeling next to my dad, and down onto the loveseat, next to him.

"Maybe not," I said slowly. "I'm guessing that whatever he wants, you still haven't given to him? Or you'd be either free or dead?"

My dad winced again, but this time from what I'd said. "Yeah. I didn't—I can't. I mean, sure, I'll give him the money, now that he found me. But I can't give him the ... other thing."

"We know," Jack told him. "You stole the information about his new planned merger. With the shifters."

"What?" Thomas sounded truly terrified now. "You can't—how did you know that? This is the kind of knowledge that gets people killed. I didn't want Tess to be anywhere near it!"

"Then why did you bring all this trouble to Dead End?" Aunt Ruby's voice was sharp and a little bit shrill. "How could you put Tess in danger?"

Uncle Mike put a tray of mugs of hot tea down on the coffee table. "I'm ashamed to call you my brother, some-times, Tommy," he said, quietly. "First, you abandon your dying wife to go climb in a bottle, then you abandon your child. All these years, we never heard from you once, and now here you are. Bringing your criminal colleagues to Dead End. To Tess's front door. And now, they're after her for her ability?"

He suddenly turned and slammed his fist against the

wall, shocking all of us, except Jack, I think, who studied him with calm eyes.

"Mike," my father said. "I never would have put her in danger. I just wanted to see her—"

"I, I, I," Uncle Mike said bitterly. "It was always about you. I see two decades plus hasn't changed that. What is it you have that they want so much? Files? Some kind of ledger?"

"An encrypted thumb drive. There's no way I could open it without it self-destructing or destroying the data or something, but I'm sure the FBI has people who could figure it out." Thomas reached for a mug, but then groaned in pain. I handed him the tea and then took one for myself.

Plenty of sugar, as I'd expected. A serious crisis is always time to bring out the sugar.

I took another sip and then blew out a shaky breath. "Okay, we need a plan. Jack, Alejandro can't get here until tomorrow evening, so what do we do until then?"

My dad looked from me to Jack and back again. "Who's Alejandro?"

"Special Agent Alejandro Vasquez, with the P-Ops division of the FBI," Jack said. "He's a friend."

"You're friends with someone from P-Ops?" Disbelief was harsh in my dad's voice. "How did that happen?"

"How it happened is Jack's reputation is so stellar that Alejandro actually wanted Jack to be his new partner," I snapped. "He's helped us out before, and after I played him the recording of O'Sullivan threatening me—"

"The *what*?" Uncle Mike shouted.

Aunt Ruby, who'd been pacing, suddenly collapsed into her reading chair with a soft cry.

We filled them all in on everything that had happened since we'd first run into the mobsters at Beau's.

"So, now, you tell us where that thumb drive is, so we can give it to Alejandro and crush these people," I concluded.

But my dad was shaking his head. "No. Not until I hear what they're offering. Tess, you don't understand. I could go away as an accessory to so many of his crimes, but I was just caught up in it. It wasn't my fault. After your mom ... after she died, I went on a six-year bender. When I woke up, I was in debt to some of Sully's gang, and I had no way to pay it. They were going to collect or kill me."

He cleared his throat and looked anywhere but at me. "I started working for them, to pay my debt. Not bad stuff—no violence," he hastened to add. "Just low-level bookie stuff. I was strictly small time. But recently ... Recently I started to see things that were so bad I couldn't hide my head in the sand any longer. I couldn't look the other way one more time. And if this shifter plan comes to pass, it will be the worst thing that could ever happen to the entire northeast part of the United States. Maybe worse, because others will take their cue from Sully's success and try to do the same thing elsewhere."

He reached out a hand to me. Let it fall. "I just wanted to make a difference. Do something you could be proud of, for the first time in my life. So I could finally come home and get to know my baby girl."

I shoved the mug at Jack, jumped up off the couch, and ran down the hallway, never stopping until I was on the back porch. Seconds later, Jack flipped off the porch light and followed me out into the dark.

"I'm sorry, Tess. You can't be out here alone, and the light spotlighted you for any long-range scopes. We don't know where O'Sullivan and his men are now. Your dad told me that they dumped him out of the truck about a mile down the road and told him to get the thumb drive or they 'd go after you, next."

I tried to laugh, but only a croaking noise came out. "Would he even care? Is he even able to care about anyone but himself?"

"Tess—"

"No! It's true. And he's my *father*. What if I'm like him? What if I turn out to be a weak, selfish monster?"

Jack pulled me into his arms and refused to let go. When I leaned against him and started to cry, he stroked my back and held me closer. It was so tempting to lean into his strength—to just stay there forever.

But we had plans to make.

"If he won't let Susan take him into protective custody," I began.

"You know he won't."

"Then we have to protect him until Alejandro gets here."

"Agreed. Your house has the most defensible position, since it's back at the end of that dirt road. I can call the boys, too."

I took a deep breath. "Okay. Now comes the hard part."

"Convincing your father to come with us?"

"Convincing Uncle Mike to stay here."

13

I n the end, Jack convinced Uncle Mike to stay home by the simple method of pointing to Aunt Ruby, who was pale and a little shaky, in spite of doing her best to keep her strong face on for me.

"I need you to protect her here, so I can focus on Tess, sir. The boys are coming out, and you know who they are and what they can do."

Uncle Mike reluctantly nodded. He knew about our friends in the swamp, all of whom had served in the military. All of whom had come home from the Middle East with various forms of PTSD. They had a good swamp boat tour business going now, and things were getting better for them, but they were loyal to a fellow soldier and would do anything for Jack.

Other than the slight upside-down-into-the-gator-pit problem, I knew they'd do anything for me, too. So did Uncle Mike.

But he wasn't happy about it.

He pulled me into a fierce hug. "You stay indoors and stay safe, you hear me? We can't lose you."

"You're not going to lose me," I promised. "And I have the rifle you gave me."

He snorted. "Except you can't hit anything you shoot at with it."

"Wrong."

He looked at me, and then at Jack.

Jack nodded. "She's been practicing. She's damn near a sharpshooter at twenty-five yards, and you can be sure I won't let anyone get closer to her than that."

I hugged Aunt Ruby, who promised to look after Lou for the night, and then we began the painful process of getting my injured father out the door.

~

We took Jack's truck, and the drive was tense.

"Like clowns in a circus," I murmured, and both of them looked at me.

"*In tents*. Get it?"

Neither of them laughed. I must not have told it right.

By the time we got to my house, I was ready to jump out of my skin. We hadn't seen anybody on the road, but Jack assured me that Lucky and the Fox twins were following us in stealth mode.

"If you can't see them, then O'Sullivan's men can't see them," he said, and it made sense, so I leaned back in the seat and took deep breaths, trying not to hyperventilate, until we got home.

We put my father, who was barely able to walk, in the guest room, and I made him take a pain pill with some water. He fell asleep so fast it made me wonder, again, just what O'Sullivan had done to him.

"I want to hurt him," I said quietly, standing at the

doorway and watching my father move restlessly under the light blanket.

"Your dad?" Jack was a shadow in the dark. He'd insisted no lights until we were sure the perimeter was secure.

"No."

"Trust me. I want to hurt *him*, too. And we will. We'll hurt him by getting him and his entire organization locked up in a dark hole with the previous Dead End sheriff."

I turned and headed toward the kitchen. "I need some coffee, if we're going to be up all night."

"Sounds like a good idea." He followed me into the kitchen and started making coffee when I stopped suddenly and forgot what I'd been about to do.

"I don't recognize my life," I told him. "Ever since ..."

"Ever since I came into it?" His voice was as dark as the shadows surrounding him. "Maybe I should leave, too, once we get past this crisis. I don't want to bring violence or danger into your life, Tess, and mine has been shrouded in both of those for so long I don't know if I can ever escape it."

"No!" I whirled to face him. "I was going to say ever since Jeremiah died, but that was about Sheriff Lawless and the Kowalskis. Nothing that has happened has been because you caused it, Jack. You have only been a friend and—and—and someone I don't really know how I ever lived without."

Confessions made in the dark don't count, right? When someone can't see the emotion that must be naked on my face, then I won't have to live with the consequences if he rejects it.

Rejects me.

The silence stretched out until I thought I'd scream, but then finally he spoke.

"You'll never have to live without me again, if you don't

want to," he said roughly, and I followed the truth of his words across the room, until I stood in front of him.

"It's not looking good for our date," I whispered. "But maybe you could kiss me now, anyway."

His sharply indrawn breath was my only answer at first, but then ... "Are you sure?"

"Very sure." I put my hands on his shoulders and raised my face to his. "Please."

It was almost as if the word broke something in his control. Jack wrapped his arms around me, pulled me against his hard, muscular body, and took my mouth with all the heat and skill and passion I'd known he'd possess.

And I kissed him back.

I raised my hands to his face and pulled him closer, and I kissed him until my knees went wobbly and the world around us disappeared. Until it was just the two of us, alone in the dark, wondering why we hadn't done this before.

Why we didn't do it all the time.

Until my father limped into the room and turned on a light.

"What the hell are you doing with my daughter?"

I rested my forehead on Jack's chest and started laughing. "You picked a heck of a time to start playing Dad."

"Turn off that light. You're making us clear targets," Jack commanded.

My dad switched off the light. "You're not good enough for her," he said bitterly. "And I ought to know about not being good enough for Tess."

"That's the difference between us," Jack said. "At least I'm trying to be."

"I'll decide who's good enough for me," I told them both. "And now, I'm going to take a shower. Feel free to argue amongst yourselves while the bad guys are out there hunting us down."

By the time I got out of the shower, put on an old T-shirt and shorts to sleep in, and went back in my bedroom, Jack was in tiger form and standing on my bed, looking out my window.

"You're lucky that's a sturdy bed."

He tilted his head and then jumped off the bed and headed for the door.

"You're going on patrol?"

He dipped his head.

"Is it safe for me to sleep for a few hours? I got very little rest last night, and I'm almost too exhausted to even think."

He turned and nudge me toward the bed, which made me laugh, in spite of everything. "I get it. Go. Wake me up if there's anything or anyone going on out there."

He turned back toward the door.

"Hey. Jack. Next time you want to avoid the 'let's talk about that kiss' conversation, you can just say so. You don't have to shift shapes to get out of any feelings talk."

Before I could think of anything else to say about it, he was gone.

I walked over and touched the Donald Duck that I'd moved from the couch to my dresser. "Men, right?"

Donald said nothing.

"For a duck, you're kind of a chicken," I told him, and then I fell onto the bed and immediately into a deep, dreamless sleep.

When I woke up, the sun was shining through my window, and it took me a moment to reorient my brain to the big, honking pile of problems facing me. I glanced at my phone and got the first good news in awhile: a text from Susan that said O'Sullivan and his goons had left town.

"Another day, another dollar, Donald. I guess I'd better get ready for work."

Donald again said nothing.

Jack, on the other hand, who sounded like he was in the kitchen, did say something.

He said *no*.

~

"*Y*ou are not the boss of me," I said, like a big dang grownup. "I told you what Susan said. They're gone. They gave up.

Jack said something about danger.

I ignored him. If he could kiss me like that and then avoid me for the rest of the night, I was certainly capable of ignoring his warnings that it was too dangerous to go to work.

"Look," I finally said. "Susan said they're gone. She said she had a deputy follow them clear across I-4 to I-95, and then a hundred miles up 95. In an unmarked car. Just to be sure. They're *gone*, Jack. And if I stayed home from work every time there's even a hint of danger, I'd be bankrupt."

He had no answer to that.

"Thomas, are you ready?"

My father—who was feeling even worse today in the grand tradition of 'the morning after,' according to Jack, my father himself, and even Lucky, who'd come in for a cup of coffee, shot one look at Thomas, and said, "Dude. Ouch" before heading home—slowly and painfully stood from the kitchen table and nodded.

"Are you sure you don't want to go to the doctor and get checked out?"

A smile touched his lips but didn't quite reach his eyes.

"No, I don't need a doctor. It's just a surfeit of bruises and stupidity. I'll need to heal both of those on my own."

A wave of longing swept through me. I wanted to spend the day with him. I wanted a chance to get to know him, outside the craziness he'd brought with him. In spite of everything he'd done and hadn't done, he was still my dad.

"And you'll still be at Uncle Mike's when I get off work?"

This time, the smile reached his eyes. "I promise. Go to work. We'll catch up at dinner. I'm not going anywhere."

Jack walked up behind me and tugged a strand of my hair. "I've got him. I'll take him to Mike and Ruby's, and you can go to work. It will be easier for him to climb into my truck than your car."

The idea of my poor, bruised, father contorting himself to get in the Mustang made *me* wince. "Okay. Thanks. I'll see you later, then. Both of you. Jack, please thank everyone again for me."

Sadly, when I got to the shop, the Doltar was still there, blocking the center aisle.

"Got any advice for me today, Doltar the Magnificent?"

Doltar said nothing. He didn't light up, either.

"Fickle," I told him and then headed in the back to start more coffee.

When I came back out front, Doltar was lit up like the cockpit of a 747, and a sturdy-looking man with a shaved head was walking all around it, smiling and stroking the wood of the cabinet.

"Good morning," I called out, before walking behind the counter. "Are you interested in the Doltar?"

"Hey, Tess. This is fantastic! What would you ask for something like this?"

Hey, Tess?

"Oh, have you been in the shop before?" I know people

liked to think that I could memorize all the faces that had ever shown up in my shop, but it was impossible. There were hundreds—thousands—of them, and just one of me.

He whirled around to face me, his eyes widening. "Don't tell me you don't recognize me without my suit! Tess, it's me. Bob. Bob Galianakis."

Bob ... "Blue! I'm sorry, I didn't recognize you at first. You look so much different out of costume."

He grinned. "Yeah, I get that. I stopped by to tell you that we got the job!"

"That's fantastic! Congratulations!"

"Yeah, I'd give you a hug, but, well, we found out about you." His mouth drooped in a very clown-like way, which fascinated me for a second until I realized he was feeling sheepish or bad about 'finding out' about me.

I sighed. "Gossip or research?"

He stared at his feet. "Gossip, I guess. We stopped for donuts on the way out of town the other day, and somebody mentioned we'd been at your shop, and somebody there asked if we'd touched you, and ... it just went from there."

"Well. Okay." I never knew what to say in these situations. I usually felt like people were waiting for me to demonstrate my 'freaky' powers, just not in a way that affected them personally. But with Blue—Bob—it didn't feel like that, which was kind of nice.

"Anyway, I wanted to thank Jack personally, but nobody answered at his place." He pointed a thumb at our adjoining door. "I called, but he didn't answer his phone, either."

"Yeah, he's not big on phones. Or thanks, for that matter."

Bob laughed. "I got that the other day. Anyway, listen. We figured out a way to say thanks that might mean something more. We've lined up a benefit gig. We're going to do a show in the Dead End town square this evening, donations only, and all proceeds go to the library here in town."

Doltar, lurking ominously behind Bob, suddenly lurched into full-on lights and action life. Bob jumped, and I shook my head.

"Here we go."

Doltar opened his plastic mouth. "Pick a card, Pick any card."

A single card slid out of the slot.

Bob and I looked at each other and shrugged.

"Guess you get to pick that one,"

"You pick it," he said.

"I already tried that. It won't let me take a card that isn't meant for me."

The clown looked at the fortune teller. The fortune teller looked at the clown. They both looked at me.

This had the makings of a great joke, but I didn't know where it would go from there.

I rolled my eyes. "Watch." I slowly extended my hand toward the card, and it started to slide back into the machine.

I took my hand back, and the card slid back out.

"That is just freaky," Bob said.

I did not disagree. On the other hand, I probably had a much higher threshold for 'freaky,' after the year I'd had.

He grinned at me. "Why not?" Then he grabbed the card, flipped it over and read it, and then he stumbled back a couple of steps from the Doltar.

"What is it? Blue! What is it?"

Blue—Bob—slowly held out the card, in a hand that was shaking. This one was in an elegant script font, with an illustrated border of red balls and ribbons.

*A clown and another guy are walking
through the forest at night.
The guy says to the clown "Man, this forest is really creepy at
night". The clown says "No kidding, and I have to walk all the
way back by myself."*

"That's ... oddly specific." I didn't know whether to put the card back in the machine or tear it up, salt it, and burn it, like you did for black magic.

"And oddly pinpointed. How did he know I was a clown?" Bob's face was pale, and this time it had nothing to do with makeup.

"It must have been a coincidence," I reassured him.

That my creepy machine, which was still *not plugged in*, just gave a clown a creepy clown joke. Sure, let's call that a coincidence.

"Are you still interested in buying it?"

The color slowly returned to his face. "Maybe. We kind of like odd things. Let me get together with the group and see what we'd be willing to bid. What are you asking?"

"I don't know yet. But the more unusual it becomes, the more I can ask. There are collectors out there who are crazy for the wildly unusual with a touch of the magical."

Bob, who'd been reaching out to touch it, yanked his hand away. "Magic?"

I couldn't lie to him. "Could be. As you can see, it's not plugged in, and Jack says there isn't a backup battery. So, who knows?"

Bob backed away from the Doltar, but I could tell he was intrigued. I'd learned early on to read the customers.

"Maybe," he finally said. Then he smiled at me. "Coming tonight?"

"I wouldn't miss it!"

"Later, Tess. Please tell Jack if you see him. Also, you might warn him that he's going to be getting a flood of crayon drawings from the kids at the hospital saying thanks."

Awww.

Maybe I'd frame a few for his office. He currently had all bare walls, a bare desk top, and bare book shelves, except for a framed picture of Shelley driving the airboat, a huge smile on her face and the wind in her hair.

About an hour and five or six customers later, I texted Aunt Ruby to see how my father was doing.

Resting. Are you coming over for dinner again?

Why don't you come to my place? And then we can go see the clowns.

My phone rang two seconds later, as expected. I told her about the clowns and the benefit, and we made plans to go together. She offered to make pies for dinner, and I accepted, because *Yes!*, and then the bells over my door chimed, so I told her I'd see her later.

Jack walked in, carrying donuts, and all my lady hormones that had woken up and started singing during *That Kiss* the night before tuned up for a concert.

Down, ladies.

"Did you see Bob on your way in?"

"Bob who?"

I blinked. "How easily you forget the man you handed fifty thousand dollars to so recently."

"Oh." He grinned. "Blue. Yeah, in the parking lot. He invited us to a benefit show, so I invited him to dinner."

"Oh. But—I was going to have a barbecue at my house."

"Right." Jack tapped on the Doltar's wooden cabinet. "I invited him to your house."

"Sure. Wait. What?" I stared at him. "Jack. We're going to need to talk about boundary issues. You invited Blue to my house without even asking me?"

"No."

"Oh." I was getting confused. Maybe not enough coffee.

"I invited all seven of them. Plus the boys."

"You're lucky you brought donuts."

14

I shoved Jack out the door to buy more groceries. A *lot* more groceries, if we were going to have ten—*eleven*, I shot a quick text off to Molly—eleven more people than I'd planned. He insisted on paying, this time, and I let him, considering his wild clown-inviting ways.

Then I texted Aunt Ruby to bring Lou with her. I'd missed my sweet cat the night before. She liked to curl up with me at night and hiss at Jack when he slept over in tiger form on the rug next to my bed.

Just like her namesake, Lieutenant Uhura, Lou feared nothing.

I spent some time talking to some of my Saturday regulars who stopped by, all of them marveling at the Doltar (who stayed silent, for a change), Windexed my glass counters, and took in a few items in pawn. (A laptop, an Xbox, and a taxidermied raccoon playing a tiny fiddle).

Obviously items in pawn were not for sale, so they went in the vault, but I kept the raccoon out so he could keep Fluffy and the Jackalope company. As I was writing a *NOT*

FOR SALE tag to put on its foot, I missed Eleanor and her lovely handwriting, which made me reach for my phone again and text her to invite the two of them to dinner, too.

Then I texted Jack to tell him I'd added three more to the dinner count, and to buy accordingly. He sent me back a photo of his Super Target cart packed to the brim with meat.

Fruit and vegetables, too, you lunatic carnivore!

He sent back a frowny face emoji.

The world was getting curiouser and curiouser, when rebel leader tiger shifters were texting emojis. Which made me think of another question.

I texted Jack again.

Do Cheshire cats actually exist?

Not that I've seen, but I wouldn't discount anything after I saw Siberian unicorns on Atlantis.

I read that message twice, and then I put my phone away.

"Top *that,* Doltar."

Doltar, apparently, could not.

I rewarded myself for all my industriousness with a second donut. When it hit noon and the shop was empty, decided to close up for the weekend.

The advantage of owning my own business was that I could set my own hours.

The *disadvantage* of owning my own business was that I could set my own hours. Any more weeks like this one, and I'd be going bankrupt.

But it was a rainy Saturday afternoon, which historically meant almost nobody came out to the shop, so I didn't feel that guilty about closing up at lunchtime. I locked up and headed home, where I walked right past the vacuum cleaner and climbed straight back into my bed.

· An hour and a half later, I woke up to the sound of a tiger singing in my kitchen.

Well, technically, it was Jack in human form singing and —darn him—he had a great voice. I lay there and listened to him sing along with my Elvis playlist until I realized *A Little Less Conversation* was making me think of action and satisfaction and that kiss.

Oops.

I jumped out of bed, brushed my scary hair back out of my face, changed into shorts and a relatively nice T-shirt that asked people to support the Humane Society, and headed out to find out what Jack Elvis Shepherd was up to.

I tried sneaking down the hall, so I could surprise him for a change, but he wasn't kidding about superior tiger hearing.

He still had his back to me when he waved hello. "Come on in and help me figure out where to put all this stuff."

"Holy cow!"

My entire kitchen was covered with stuffed-to-the-brim canvas totes.

"Did you buy out the entire store?"

He looked around and shrugged. "I wasn't sure what people would want, so I bought some of everything."

"No kidding." I walked around, glancing into bags, before I started unpacking. "Horseradish, yellow mustard, brown mustard, ketchup, barbecue sauce—three varieties, and mayonnaise. So, this is the condiment bag?"

"That's one of them."

Oh, boy.

"All this mustard is making me want a sandwich. You?"

He grinned at me. "Really? Have you met me?"

I made sandwiches, and we ate while we unpacked, but

there was no way all that meat would fit in my refrigerator. Jack said he had it covered, and he ran out to the truck and brought in a huge plastic Coleman Cooler, already partially filled with ice.

"I need to buy you a freezer. Or a second refrigerator," he said absently, as he loaded meat into the cooler.

I stopped mid-bite. "Um, no. I don't know how it is in your world, but here you don't buy major appliances for a woman unless you're already married."

He stopped what he was doing and gave me a speculative look. "So, if we get married, I can buy you a second fridge *and* a freezer *and* a new grill?"

I choked on my sandwich and took a big drink of water to wash it down. Then I went and switched on the vacuum to drown out the sound of his chuckles.

~

Three hours later, my cat was home, and my house was filled with family, friends, food, and laughter. Everything was right with my world. I reluctantly decided against a third piece of pie, because I didn't own any elastic-waisted shorts (I needed to remedy that in a hurry), but Jack swooped in and saved me from it.

"You love this, don't you? The house full of people, family barbecues. Pie."

I leaned against his shoulder. "Who doesn't love pie? And what about you? Is it too much for you? You're the one who invited the clowns, after all."

He smiled at me. "I'm surprised to be saying this, but I do enjoy it. I don't understand how you turned me into a people person, after so many years of being mostly alone."

"How could you be alone with all those soldiers around? And Quinn?"

I was more relieved than I'd admit that he didn't get that tightness around his eyes anymore at the sound of her name. She'd meant a lot to him, and then she'd gone and married someone else.

I was going to have to thank her for that one day.

"That wasn't about fun and barbecues. That was about survival and battles and avoiding death."

My father, who was moving around a little better, walked into the kitchen and glared at Jack. "Don't you have some-place to be?"

Uncle Mike followed him in. "Ha! Jack will be wherever the dessert is, count on it."

"He can stop looking at my daughter like she *is* dessert," my dad grumbled, making my face turn hot.

"Did I tell you about Owen?" Uncle Mike grinned at me. "Tess used to date a dentist. You would have liked him. Bored the stuffing out of me every time he came over, but definitely not the type to get into dangerous situations."

Thomas perked up. "Used to date?"

"She's not dating anybody now," Uncle Mike said nonchalantly, deliberately not looking at me or Jack.

Jack put his arm around me and smiled. His "lots of teeth" smile. "Wanna bet?"

I shoved his arm away, suddenly fed up with all of them. "I am not sure how my mobster father thinks he can comment on the people I date. Except, wait. Does that make me a mob princess? Can I be on a reality show?"

I sashayed over to the sink and put down my cup, and then batted my eyelashes at them and put on a high-pitched voice. "Ooh, are you really Tiffany Corleone? Who does your giant hair? Do you spend Saturday nights making out with Made Men?"

My dad flinched, but Jack and Uncle Mike roared with laughter.

"She's got you there, Tommy," Uncle Mike said, when he could catch his breath.

I turned on Jack. "And you. Ready to tell me about Cleveland yet?"

My dad sucked in a breath. "Cleveland? That was *you*?"

Jack said nothing.

"What? What about Cleveland?"

My father just shook his head. "I can't talk about it."

I stared at them in disbelief. "You're all a bunch of clowns."

Orange, who was a gorgeous, curvy blonde when not in costume, popped in from the back porch. "You called?"

"Um, no. I wasn't talking about actual clowns. I'm sorry, I—"

"You know, Tess, that kind of anti-clown bias is really unacceptable."

"I'm sorry," I said humbly. "I won't do it again."

"See that you don't. And this pie? Is magnificent." She held up a plate that held the slightest trace that blueberry pie had once been on it. "Any chance I can get the recipe?"

"I bet you can. Come meet my Aunt Ruby."

I nodded toward the living room, and we left the annoying men in my life to each other. Served them right.

When I finally made my way over to where Molly and Lucky were sitting on the porch swing, eating pie and chatting, I gave my best friend a big hug and squeezed in between the two of them.

"Boy, do I have a lot to tell you," I said.

Molly, a petite, tattooed, force of nature who was also a rock star, had been my best friend since the first day of kindergarten. We'd been there for each other through every episode, both bad and good, in our lives, and I didn't like that we spent so much time apart now that I was a business owner and she was touring with her indie rock band, Scarlett's Letters.

But I was so proud of her and happy for her success. She'd had major record label interest and was in the process of deciding whether to go with a big company or stay indie. I'd been worried when Dice, bass guitarist for Scarlett's Letters, had been accused of murder, thinking it would hurt their chances for a record deal, but Molly said that the PR people loved it, because bad girl rockers were a huge draw.

I didn't understand this at all, but that was okay. I didn't have to understand it. I just had to support her.

"I know. Lucky has been filling me in," she said. "We need a girls' spa day to catch up."

I sighed. "That sounds unbelievably good. Maybe next Sunday? I'm not sure what will happen tomorrow, or when my father is leaving ..."

Her eyes widened. "How are you holding up with that? Not the mob crap, but the emotional stuff?"

I felt tears threaten. She was the only one who'd asked me about that. "Harder than I could have ever expected when I imagined him coming back."

She knew. I'd talked to her about my dad coming back a lot when we were kids, back when I secretly thought he might be a spy or an astronaut or a time traveler, and that's why he couldn't come back to see me.

A mobster had never been anywhere near my list.

Live and learn.

"Okay, everyone." Aunt Ruby walked out on the porch,

clapping her hands. "Time to go. We need to get the clowns downtown, so they can get ready for their show, and we can get front-row seats."

"We made sure to reserve seats in the front row for all of you," Purple—Melvin—said, walking out behind her. "After all, this whole show is thanks to Jack and Tess."

Everybody started applauding when Jack walked outside, and he froze with a tiger-in-the-headlights expression. The man could face rampaging vampires and armed mobsters, but people expressing gratitude scared the crap out of him.

I kind of liked that in a man.

I hopped up and went to rescue him. "Let's get going, folks."

"We'll help you clean up," Bob said, but I waved him away.

"Nope. Jack loves doing dishes, for some reason, so we've got it covered. You need to go! Don't want to disappoint any kids, do you?"

That got them going. "Don't disappoint the children" was probably a major clown tenet.

I waved goodbye to everyone, avoiding hugs from a couple of the clowns who weren't thinking about my ability, and then locked the door and followed Jack down the steps.

"I can drive," I said, looking longingly at my sweet new car—a gift from my grandmother—that I hadn't been driving much lately.

"You could," Jack said slowly. "But there will be a lot of people downtown, and with your little parking issue ..."

"Fine." He was right. I had a minor spatial or perspective issue that made me terrible at parking. Or at least that was what I'd been claiming since everybody quit believing me when I blamed it on defective mirrors.

"But hurry up. I'm dying to hear what seven clowns playing ukuleles sound like," I said with a wicked grin.

Ha. Take *that*, Mr. Superior Tiger Hearing.

Jack flinched.

I hummed all the way to the park.

15

J ack had predicted it. The park and all of downtown Dead End (which is all of five square blocks) were packed with people excited to see the clowns. Some of the kids were even dressed up like clowns, in spite of scary movies. We parked by Mellie's Bakery and walked over to the city square, where hundreds of people were scattered on lawn chairs, blankets, and even golf carts, chatting with friends and enjoying the evening.

The afternoon rain had cooled the August air off to a balmy 85 or so, which was practically a cold front for us this time of year. I pointed to a row of chairs blocked off with red ribbons right in front of the portable stage. "I bet that's for us! There's Aunt Ruby and Uncle Mike with Molly and Lucky."

I didn't see the clowns, but that made sense, because they'd be getting ready somewhere. We took our seats and in only a few minutes, Lorraine jumped by us and hopped up onto the stage.

"Welcome, welcome!"

Everybody applauded, so she took a bow, and we all laughed.

"We're delighted to have the famous Somersaulting Seven, now a featured act with the Tampa New Performing Circus, visit us here in Dead End and put on this benefit. Proceeds go to the library, which needs the help since the roof leaked over the children's collection. I'm passing jars around now. Feel free to fill 'em up."

Everybody applauded again and pulled out their wallets.

"And I'll be in touch for hurricane prep signups, so be expecting me," Lorraine boomed through the microphone, to scattered applause and a little bit of booing.

"I know, I know, but we go through this every year. And we've got some big ones on the horizon, I hear. But enough about work and disaster. Please put your hands together for the Somersaulting Seven!"

She hurried off the stage to the sound of loud applause and whistles, and, from somewhere behind the stage, circus music started to play. Then our friends the clowns somersaulted onto the stage, proving they deserved their name.

They were *terrific*.

I laughed and cheered with everyone else as they did an intricate and yet funny tumbling routine which made it look like Purple was the clumsiest clown on the planet, when in fact he was executing very difficult, precise moves to pull it off. The others had their timing down so perfectly that the entire routine was brilliant.

Just when I didn't know how it could get any better, they brought the dogs on stage.

Big dogs, little dogs, and medium-sized dogs. There were at least a dozen, and they all wore tutus and performed with the clowns. Some of the dogs jumped over and under their human partners, some rode tiny bicycles, and one tiny poodle-mix walked across a tightrope on her hind legs.

It was so amazing, and we loved every minute of it. I even caught Jack relaxing his constant vigilance and enjoying the show. He reached over and took my hand, and we sat shoulder to shoulder, laughing and cheering, letting the tension and stress and fear of the week drain away.

When the show ended, I noticed that my dad was gone from his seat and looked around to see him walking slowly toward the direction of City Hall, which always left its restrooms open during events.

Bob took the microphone, and I turned back to the stage.

"Thank you. You've been a wonderful audience. We always like to let everyone know that each one of our dogs was originally a rescue dog, and we've adopted them from shelters across the country. Adopt, don't shop, and you, too, can find a Fifi," he waved to the wire-walking poodle, who bowed, to great applause. "Or a Beauregard." He pointed to a very chubby pug, who'd mostly just ridden around in a wagon pushed by a Golden Retriever mix, but who'd looked adorable doing it. The pug wagged his donut tail, and everyone cheered again.

"Now, for a special thanks. We walked into Tess Callahan's pawn shop with seven ukuleles—not a sight she sees every day—and she was going to help us out, in spite of there not being a huge market in Dead End for them." He grinned when everybody laughed, and all seven of the clowns played a song.

The pug made a show of covering his ears with his little paws, and everybody cracked up.

Orange stepped forward. "And then, a man with a very good heart helped us out and also made a big donation to the children's hospital where we were headed to perform. So, we decided that the best way to say thanks, other than keeping him anonymous, as he wished, was to pay it forward. We hope you enjoyed our show, and we hope you empty those pockets into the jars for the library!"

With a flourish, all the clowns and even all the dogs bowed, and then they danced off the stage. I jumped up and led the crowd in a standing ovation.

"That was amazing!" I couldn't stop smiling.

"You're amazing," Jack murmured into my ear. "Thank you for this. I'm going to go help Lorraine collect the jars. Back in a flash."

I watched him stride through the crowd, probably not even realizing how people just naturally moved out of his way, and then someone jostled me from behind.

"Excuse me," I automatically started to say, but something hard poked into my ribs, and a man with a harsh New York accent snarled in my ear.

"Shut it. I have a message for you from my boss."

"Who are you?"

He slammed the gun—it had to be a gun—into my ribs again, harder. "I said shut up. We have Thomas O'Malley, or Callahan, or whatever the hell he calls himself. Your daddy. If you want him to live, come to the house under construction just down the dirt road from your place within the next thirty minutes and bring what Tommy stole from us. If you don't show up, Daddy dies. If you bring your tiger friend, they both die. We're watching from the roof, so we'll know if you bring anybody. And we'll do things to you that make you wish you were dead. Bring what we want, and we let you both go. You got me?"

I suddenly shifted and reached out to touch him, but he

jumped back, his eyes widening in fear. "Don't you touch me. I know about you, you witch."

"I'm not a witch, but if you hurt my father, you'll *wish* you only had to deal with a witch," I threatened. An empty threat, but he didn't know that.

He scowled. "Just bring it. And hurry up."

"I don't know what he stole."

The man started to walk off, but then stopped and looked back at me. His smile was filled with so much pure evil I felt like vomiting. "I guess you better figure it out. You have half an hour."

Then he disappeared into the crowd.

Damn it, Dad. Where did you put that stupid thumb drive? And don't mobsters today know about the cloud?

I started walking, not even knowing where I was going, and then I saw someone I knew very well and walked right up to him.

"Hey. I need a ride to my house. And I have a problem you may be able to help me with."

"Jack told me about the Doltar. I'd love to see it and find out what makes it tick," my driver said.

"Sure, but good luck with that. So far, it has refused to let me read cards, turned on with no visible power source, and told Jack to BEWARE THE POULTRY. Also, you have to ride in the trunk."

All the way home, I wracked my brain for where my dad might have hidden that thumb drive. If he'd put it somewhere in the barn or in Uncle Mike's house, there was no way I'd find it in time.

Then suddenly, just as I drove past Carlos's house and the three SUVs parked beside it, that niggling sensation in my brain started to zing, and I followed the thought back to its source, everything from the past few days jumbling together in my mind.

Beware the poultry.

Poultry.

Chickens.

"For a duck, you're kind of a chicken."

For a duck ...

I knew where the thumb drive was.

~

I made a quick phone call, and then, exactly thirty minutes from the time the thug had accosted me at the show, I was standing in front of Carlos Gonzalez's new house, holding a thumb drive in one hand and a key in the other.

That's when five thugs with guns surrounded me.

16

I had never been more scared in my life, even with my secret weapon hiding in the trees somewhere nearby and help—once he calmed down and quit roaring—on the way.

But this was my father, and I wasn't going to let him die.

"In there," one of the goons said, motioning with his gun to the front of the house. The front door wasn't on yet, but the new roof was. The second floor framing wasn't yet done, though, so I looked up into the darkness of the vaulted ceiling and saw only shadows.

I lifted my chin and marched through the door, only to find that O'Sullivan stood next to my father, who was tied to a chair and gagged with a bandanna.

"Really? Tied to a chair? Watch too many movies, O'Sullivan? Are you planning to tie me to the train tracks next?"

I was being mouthy on purpose, not because I had a death wish, but because my backup needed time to get in place.

O'Sullivan laughed at me. "Feisty little brat, aren't you? Too bad your daddy never had a fraction of your backbone.

He could have risen high in the organization, instead of being a worthless drunk and a low-rent bookie."

"Better a bookie than a murderous thug," I shot back.

The amusement drained out of O'Sullivan's face, leaving his eyes empty again.

The eyes of a killer.

"Where's my money?"

I held out the key. "It has the bank name stamped on it. I'm guessing it's a safe deposit box."

My father was trying to shout and fighting against the ropes, but O'Sullivan and I both ignored him. The monster clearly wasn't worried about him, and I didn't dare take my eyes off the biggest evil in the room.

He held out his hand, and I dropped the key into it, careful not to touch him. I didn't like to touch snakes, either, and I definitely didn't want to see how he was going to die unless I had no choice.

"And the other thing?"

"I'll tell you where it is after you let my father go," I said, pretending to be calm and cool, like I conducted negotiations at gunpoint all the time.

O'Sullivan took out his gun and pointed it at my dad's head. "Change of plans. Give me the thumb drive, or I'll shoot your daddy in the head right now."

"You promised you'd let him go!"

O'Sullivan rolled his eyes, and the goons behind me laughed.

"I'm a criminal. I lie. Get over it. Now hand over the damn thumb drive. This is your last chance."

I really didn't have any choice. It's not like I really was a witch and could shoot spells at them. I was a one-trick pony, and I was about to play my only trick.

I pulled the drive out of my pocket and held it out. This time, I made O'Sullivan come to me.

When his hand reached out, I grabbed it.

And I held on when he tried to knock me down.

Only when he backhanded me across the face did I finally let go of his hand and sink to my knees on the wooden floor. And then I looked up at him, and I smiled.

"I know how you're going to die, Mr. O'Sullivan. Are you interested in that knowledge?"

I wasn't lying, either. I'd seen his death, and I let the knowledge of what I'd seen fill my eyes.

He backed away from me, wild-eyed and gasping. "No. No, you bitch, I don't want to know ... Yes! Yes, tell me, damn you." He aimed his gun at my dad again, but I shook my head.

"Not this time. You'll kill us anyway. So this time we play it my way," I said, feeling oddly sure I was echoing dialogue from an old movie.

"You let him go, and then I'll tell you what I saw. You can take precautions. Take it or leave it."

He turned his gun to me. "Then I'll shoot you, instead."

My brain wanted me to start shrieking, but I forced myself to remain strong. Didn't allow myself to cry or throw up from sheer terror.

"Go ahead," I said, forcing myself up off the floor instead of curling up in a ball. "And then you'll never know what's coming until the day you actually die."

I could almost see the crazed calculations going on in his weaselly mind. He wanted to know, but he was terrified to know. It was the same reaction any normal person had to my ability, magnified by maybe a thousand due to his criminal lifestyle.

Finally, he caved. "Let him go," he barked at his thugs, who looked shocked but still did what they were told.

"Dad," I said urgently. "Look at me. Run to my house. Get in my house and lock the door. There's pie in the kitchen."

He screamed behind his gag, but the goons manhandled him out of the house and shoved him down. I cried out, but O'Sullivan grabbed my arm before I could run out to him.

"He's fine. Now tell me what you saw."

"First, I believe this is yours." I dropped the thumb drive into his hand, but at this point he almost didn't care about his precious information. He was too busy losing his mind about what I knew about his death.

But then reality intruded, and his piggy eyes narrowed even further. "Did you make a copy?"

"How was I supposed to copy an encrypted thumb drive? I'm a pawnshop owner, not a hacker," I said scornfully.

He knew the strength of his encryption, so he just smiled and shoved the drive into his pocket.

"Now. Tell me."

Instead, I looked up. "Are there bats up there? I'm terrified of bats."

O'Sullivan, fed up with my delays, knocked me down again, this time by way of his fist in my stomach. I fell to the floor again, gasping for air. This time, the tears rushed to my eyes before I could fight them back.

It *hurt*.

I wanted this day to be over.

Jack, where are you?

O'Sullivan pointed his gun directly at my head. "Tell me, right now, or I'll shoot you in your pretty face. If you think—"

But I never got a chance to know what he was going to say, because a dark shape dropped from the rafters, knocked

O'Sullivan to the floor, and then ran back out of the house. Then a mighty roar shook the very foundations of the house, and suddenly Jack was there, next to me, and two of the thugs were down on the porch with claw marks across their bellies.

Another thug flew forward and onto his face on the floor, and Dave Wolf stepped up behind him, wielding the bat that he'd just slammed into the man's back.

And then I grabbed a two-by-four and I smashed it into the face of the thug running in from the back of the house.

"Five down, none to go?" Dave asked.

Before I could draw breath to answer that I thought there were six, my dad ran back into the house and grabbed me in a hug before I could stop him.

In one of the best developments of the entire week, I saw nothing at all about how he was going to die.

Then a shot exploded into the space, and we all ducked away from the sound. The sixth man had shown up, and he was armed.

"Step away from the boss," he snarled. "Or I'll shoot you all, starting with the girl."

Then, he simply disappeared. One minute, he was standing there pointing his gun at me, and the next minute, he literally flew into the air, screaming. We heard a sharp crack, and then his body fell to the ground. The way he landed, it was clear that his neck was broken.

Jack looked at me, but I shook my head. "Not one of mine."

A moment later, an extremely handsome man with long, dark, wavy hair and darkly tanned skin stalked into the house, holding his hands up, but it clearly wasn't in surrender. This guy was wrapped in arrogance and sheer, primal male hotness, reminding me of someone else I knew.

"Welcome to my home, Tess. I thought I should join the party, so to speak."

I grinned. "Carlos! Carlos Gonzalez. It's great to see you again. And wow, talk about good timing." I walked toward him, with some idea of hugging him or shaking his hand, but my tiger had other ideas.

Jack moved his furry self until he was standing between me and Carlos, and then he shimmered back to human. "Tess. Step away from the vampire."

"Vampire?" My mouth fell open. "Really? But Susan—"

Carlos's dark eyes turned stormy. "Yes. We will discuss this at another time."

"Well. Thank you for your help, sorry about your house —meeting here was not my idea—and welcome to the neighborhood. I'll bake you a pie!"

A real smile warmed my new neighbor's face, and suddenly I felt foolish. "Do you even eat pie?"

"Pecan?"

"Of course."

He inclined his head. "Then yes, I would greatly appreciate a pie."

Jack growled a little, and I punched his arm. "Thank my neighbor for his help."

Jack glared at me. "If you'd told me what happened, you wouldn't have needed his help."

"If I'd told you, my father would be dead."

My dad, who was silently taking this all in, stepped forward and took my hand. "I'm sorry about hugging you, Tess. Did you—"

I smiled at him. "Nope. Not a thing."

Dad blew out a sigh of relief. "I'm so glad. I don't want to know, and I didn't want you to have to go through that."

O'Sullivan, still on the ground, sat up and scowled at me. "But you said you knew about me."

"I do," I said evenly.

"I can't believe you'd give him the drive, Tess," my dad said with a hint of regret. "I mean, it's all good now, but if he'd gotten away with that—"

I laughed. "Oh. No. You didn't meet my friend who dropped out of the rafters."

I looked out into the dark and called out. "Hey, Austin! Come on in. We've got them all."

Austin, our friend, the tall, dark, and gorgeous hunk of former Army Ranger and current brilliant computer hacker, strode into the room. Jack started to laugh.

"She asked you if you could de-encrypt a flash drive, didn't she?"

"Yep. Made me ride in the trunk of my car, too, so these losers didn't see me."

"And could you? De-encrypt it?" my dad asked anxiously.

"Does a bear—" Austin looked at me. "Poop in the woods? Child's play. I've transmitted the information to my account on the dark web and also uploaded it to Alejandro at P-Ops."

I blinked. "You have Alejandro's password information?"

Austin gave me a sorrowful look. "Oh, Tess."

"Ah."

"This is all fascinating, but I have someplace to be," said the vampire, er, Carlos. "But first, I'd like to know who exactly has such a delicious scent."

It was such a vampire thing to say that a shiver ran down my spine, especially when he did a slow turn around the room, actually sniffing the air. Then he froze in place, his black gaze fixed on Dave, who stood alone next to one wall, still holding his bat.

Carlos smiled a slow, dangerous smile and stalked over to Dave, step by deliberate step. "Are you my neighbor, too?"

Dave, looking both nervous and fascinated, held out a hand. "Everybody in Dead End is your neighbor. I'm Dave Wolf. Glad to meet you."

Carlos shook his hand and then pulled Dave closer until they were face to face, practically touching. "Not yet. But you will be," he said in a deep, husky tone. Then he turned and raced out of the back door and disappeared into the night.

"Wow," Dave said, his voice a little shaky. "That was ... wow."

I looked at Jack and started laughing. "I know exactly what you mean."

My dad suddenly leaned over, grabbed O'Sullivan's hand and pulled him up off the floor, and then punched him in the face so hard he knocked him back down.

"That's for threatening my daughter, you son of a bitch."

I had to admit, I wasn't sad he did it.

Then everything happened at once. Susan and her deputies arrived at the same time that Alejandro and a P-Ops team showed up. All the law enforcement types took everybody into custody, and I was more than ready to go home, take a shower, and cuddle my cat.

I glanced at Jack. Maybe cuddle both of my cats.

When one of the P-Ops agents dragged O'Sullivan out of the room, he dragged his feet and looked back at me. "Tell me, damn you. You know, so tell me."

Jack squeezed my hand. "It's up to you."

"I know." I took a deep breath and decided. Then I walked over to the man who'd brought so much pain and trouble to my family, and I told him the absolute truth.

"You will die when you're very old."

His entire face lit up, and he shouted out his triumph. "Ha! I win! No matter what you do to me, I'm going to live to be a rich and successful old man."

I leaned forward and touched his arm, because now it didn't matter. I only ever saw a vision once. "I wasn't finished."

He stopped, mid-shout, and stared down at me with trepidation in his muddy eyes. "What?"

"You're going to die when you're very old ... in *prison*."

Jack grinned. "Have a good, long, life, O'Sullivan."

My dad started to laugh.

O'Sullivan screamed all the way to the police car.

17

Alejandro was on his way to deal with another case, but he stopped long enough to tell us that he'd love to bring his wife and come down to Florida for a vacation sometime soon. We promised to show him around all the fun places and thanked him for coming out, yet again.

"The partnership offer still stands, my friend," he told Jack, shaking his hand.

Jack shook his head. "This one was all Tess. You should ask her to be your partner."

Alejandro smiled and took my hand and kissed it. "I should be so lucky."

"Kiss my girl again, and you'll lose a hand," Jack said mildly.

"In your dreams, Shepherd," Alejandro returned.

I didn't know whether to be pleased or insulted at the 'my girl,' so I just let it go. I was too darn tired. "Come over for a drink or a piece of pie?"

Alejandro looked tempted but had to decline. "I have a

plane to catch. Soon, though. We'll drink tequila and eat pie and tell lies about our past."

"You silver-tongued federal agent, you. Is that how you won Rose?" I grinned at him.

"Not exactly. She magicked my pants off in the park and then ran away and left me there."

"That's a story—"

"You don't need to hear," Jack said, taking my hand. "Let's get your dad back to your place."

I looked around to find Dad talking to Dave. Both of them looked shell-shocked.

"Okay, everyone. Pie at my house."

Jack and I led the way on the short walk to my house, with my dad, Dave, and Austin following.

We ate pie and shared our stories, and then my dad went to shower and sleep in the guest room, Austin left to pick his brother up at the train station, Dave went home, and Jack and I sat on the couch with Lou sprawled out between us.

"That was one heck of a first date."

I narrowed my eyes. "That was *not* our first date."

"No? Are you sure? Maybe this dating thing is a bad idea after all, Tess. I don't want you to be in danger because of me."

I stood, marched into my room, grabbed The Dress, and marched back out.

Then I held the tiny, silky, shimmery, piece of red fabric up against my body and raised an eyebrow.

Jack gulped so loudly he startled Lou. "Never mind. Forget I said anything. I'll just—I'll see you tomorrow."

"You bet your butt you will," I told him. When he leaned over and tried to kiss me, I pointed to the door. "Go home. The danger is over."

"I've heard that before." Jack stretched. "I'll just sleep out here on the couch with Lou."

I shrugged. I had no problem with that.

~

*W*hen I woke up in the morning, he was gone.

~

*O*n Sunday mornings, my shop is officially closed, but I had one piece of business I was anxious to take care of. At eleven a.m., the clowns—wearing street clothes and no makeup—met me at the door.

"Junior says he'll take fifteen hundred dollars, because that covers what it cost him," I told Blue, who led the way into the shop. "And you were all amazing last night. Thank you so much for doing that!"

"Where did you take off to?"

I told them a little bit about what had happened, and they were satisfyingly impressed, and then we got down to business.

"Are you still sure you want him?"

"Absolutely," said Orange. "He belongs with us in the circus. He's too regal to sit here. No offense, Tess."

"None taken. I was thinking the same thing."

The Doltar said nothing but I truly believed he stood just a little bit straighter in his cabinet.

They gave me fifteen hundred dollars in cash from their signing bonus with the new circus, and I handed them the paperwork from Junior. I wasn't even taking a commission since I'd never officially taken Doltar into inventory.

"Well, goodbye, Doltar," I told him, when they were ready to go. "I confess, I'm going to miss you."

Lights and bells started flashing and ringing, and Doltar turned his head to look at me with his terrifying plastic eyeballs. A card slid out of the slot nearest me, but I was afraid to take it.

I'd been burned by the Doltar before.

He kept looking at me, though, and he didn't take the card back.

"Go ahead," Green urged me. "Tell us what it says."

So, I took the card and read it out loud:

BEWARE MURDER IN HURRICANE SEASON

Oh, boy.

~

*a*t seven o'clock, sharp, I kissed Lou on the head and stepped out onto the front porch when I heard Jack's footsteps.

It took nearly a full minute before he could catch his breath enough to speak, which was intensely, deliciously, satisfying, and even then he looked at me like I was a slice of pecan pie, and he was a starving man.

"You wore the red dress," he said, his eyes lit up like Christmas morning.

"I wore the red dress."

When he took my hand and an almost-electric shock raced up my skin, it finally occurred to me:

I might be in big trouble.

Respectfully Submitted,

Tiger's Eye Investigations

~

*A*re you dying to know what happens when the storm of the century—Hurricane Elvis—hits Dead End, just when Jack has to take on a dangerous new case? And what happened on that date? Preorder **EYE OF THE STORM HERE.**

Missed the beginning? Find out how it all started when a tiger, an alligator, and a redneck walked into Tess's pawnshop! Get **DEAD EYE FREE HERE!**

~

I'm thrilled to announce that the Tiger's Eye Mysteries will continue for at least fifteen books in total, and you'll be able to read the continuing adventures of Jack, Tess, and the gang for years to come!

If you want free books, the scoop on all new releases, behind-the-scenes details, and the chance to win prizes, text ALYSSADAY to 66866 (or go to my website at www.alyssaday.com) to sign up for my newsletter. I promise never to sell, fold, spindle, or mutilate your information so you will get no spam—ever—from me.

Hang out with me on Facebook! My special super-fun fan group for readers is here: https://www.facebook.com/groups/DayDreamersAlyssaDay/

You can also follow me on BookBub if you only want new release news.

Thanks again for reading—you rock!

Review it. My family hides the chocolate if I don't mention that reviews help other readers find new books, so if you have the time, please consider leaving one. I appreciate all reviews, and thank you for your time.

Try my other books! You can find excerpts of all of my books at http://alyssaday.com.

Happy reading!

Alyssa

EXCERPT FROM DEAD EYE

Excerpt from DEAD EYE, the first in the Tiger's Eye mysteries, now available FREE HERE!

A tiger, an alligator, and a redneck walked into my pawnshop.

I sighed when I realized my life had devolved into the opening line of a tired joke, but I was awfully glad to see the tiger. Maybe now we could finally get things straightened out.

And to be fair, the alligator didn't exactly walk, so much as it rolled in on a cart. It had been the unfortunate victim of some really bad taxidermy, and stared out at the world from two mismatched eyes, its mouth open in a half-hearted attempt at ferocity or, more likely, indignation about the sparkly pink scarf wrapped around its neck. It had been wearing a blue plaid scarf the last time I'd seen it. Apparently even stuffed alligators had better wardrobes than I did.

The redneck, lean and wiry in a desert-camo t-shirt and baggy khaki pants, shuffled in sideways, pushing the rolling cart and casting frequent wary glances back over his shoulder at the tiger.

Jack Shepherd was the tiger, and he had nothing at all to do with the redneck or the alligator. The pawnshop, however, was a different story. The pawnshop, according to the will my late boss—Jack's uncle Jeremiah—had left in the top drawer of his ancient desk, now belonged to Jack.

At least, fifty percent of it did. The other half was mine. I was still trying not to feel guilty about that.

"Nice to see you again, Jack," I said, and my voice was almost entirely steady. If he'd been any other man, my hormones might have perked up and taken notice. When I was sixteen, I'd certainly entertained more than a few swoony thoughts about him. Jack was maybe four inches over six feet and seriously hot. Hard muscle in all the right places, wavy bronze hair streaked with gold, and dark green eyes. He looked like trouble walking in blue jeans and a long-sleeved black shirt. Okay, so I noticed. But I knew enough about Jack to know better than to even *think* in that direction.

As if I could, anyway.

Jack walked up and held out his hand like he wanted to shake mine. I ignored it. "Tess? Tess Callahan? When did you grow up?"

"In the ten years since you've bothered to visit."

A shadow of pain crossed his face as he slowly lowered his hand, and I felt a twinge of guilt. But only a twinge. Jeremiah had waited and waited for a call from his nephew—for any word at all—but we'd only heard about what Jack was up to from unreliable news reports and shady underground sources. Jeremiah had fretted himself nearly to death, worrying.

Otis the redneck, still lurking by his alligator, was leaning forward, eager to catch every word so he could spread the news later to his buddies over coffee at Beau's. His eyes gleamed as he watched the interplay. "Tess don't shake hands, Mister. She don't let people touch her."

Right. Enough of that.

"I don't think so, Otis," I told him. "I told you last time that I wasn't taking that decrepit alligator in pawn one more time."

"Aw, come on, Tess," he whined. "One more time, that's all. I got a hunch about a good one down to the greyhound track. You gave me a hunnerd for Fluffy last time. I'll take fifty."

"Fluffy?" Jack asked. "You named a dead gator Fluffy?"

Otis glared at him. "Her name was Fluffy when she was alive, Mister, not that it's any of your business."

"When was she alive? About a century ago?" Jack nodded at the dilapidated gator coated in about an inch of dust. "And did she wear the scarf when she was alive too?"

Otis didn't even crack a smile. "Maybe *you'll* be wearing the scarf, if you don't shut your mouth, *tourist*. I'm trying to make a transaction here."

Since Otis was at least seventy years old and probably weighed a buck twenty soaking wet, I was betting that Jack didn't consider him to be much of a threat.

"Pink's totally my color," Jack said, deadpan.

I blew out a breath. Better to pay Otis, or he'd never leave. I pushed the button on the antique cash register, and the bell pealed and startled both of them. I counted out fifty dollars. "That's not a tourist, Otis. That's Jeremiah's nephew, Jack. Take this and go, please. We'll write it up later."

Otis glanced back and forth between me and Jack, started to speak, but then must have decided not to press his luck. He scurried over to the counter, snatched the money, and then almost ran out of the store.

"Maybe he'll win at the track," Jack said.

"Never happened before, but there's always a first time. Kind of like you walking into the pawnshop this decade," I said, refusing to be engaged in small talk.

"Yeah. Well, now I'm finally home, and home is looking like the ass-end of a stuffed gator," he said flatly. "Not exactly the family reunion I'd envisioned."

He had a point. No matter what the circumstances, Jack was Jeremiah's family, and I'd loved Jeremiah. Jack probably had too, in his own way. I needed to shape up and cut him some slack. Plus, according to the terms of Jeremiah's will, I would be forced to have some interaction with this man. I took a deep breath and tried to smile. "You're right. I'm sorry. Let's try again. Welcome to Dead End, Jack. It's nice to see you. I guess we're partners."

"About that. I don't want a damned pawnshop, not even half of one. Who do we need to talk to for me to sign it over to you?"

Jack looked around the shop, and I tried to see the familiar place through his eyes. It was an old building, but sparkling clean, stuffed with display cases filled with the usual pawnshop staples of jewelry, guns, and not-quite-antiques. *Collectibles*, we called them when we were being generous. *Junk*, when we weren't.

But Dead End Pawn was also home to the unusual and the bizarre, because Jeremiah's interest in the supernatural was well known to everybody within at least a five-county radius. If a vampire broke a fang and wanted to sell it, or a witch was hard up for cash and wanted to pawn a minor object of power, Jeremiah was the one they went to see.

Jeremiah, for more than forty years, and now me (except for the fangs).

But apparently not Jack.

"I can't afford to buy you out yet," I said, standing up to my full five-foot-eight and raising my chin. "And I don't want to sell. I'm hoping we can work something out."

Jack pointed to Fluffy. "Really? Not flush with cash, are you? I can't say I'm shocked."

I felt my face turning red, which I hated, since it clashed with my red hair. "Look. Otis is a special case. He was a friend of Jeremiah's, and he's always good for a loan. Not that I need to justify my business decisions to you."

He shrugged, which naturally made me notice his broad shoulders, and then he turned to look at the oversized items hanging on the back wall, which made me notice his world-class butt, and I wanted to clutch my head and moan. Just what I did *not* need. To be interested in Mr. Tall, Dark, and Dangerous—especially when he spent part of his time stalking around in his Bengal tiger form. Dating had usually been off-limits for me until I figured out how to date without actually touching the guy I was seeing, like Owen, or until my research into my nasty little eighteenth-birthday gift paid off.

The bell on the door jingled, and I saw Mrs. Gonzalez peek in. She was eighty going on a hundred and fifty and kept trying to get me to go out with her grandson. I really didn't have time for this today.

"We're closed," Jack said gently, smiling at her. "Please come back tomorrow."

I could feel my hackles rising at his nerve, but then I

glanced at the clock and it was already ten till six. Jack and I really did need to talk.

"I don't know you. You could be an axe murderer. Get out of my way and let me see Tess," she retorted, peering up at him through her curly white bangs.

Great. Next she'd call the sheriff, and I'd have to deal with *him*, which would be the cherry on the cake of my freaking life.

"This is Jeremiah's nephew," I said, hurrying over to reassure her. "We need to discuss some things, Mrs. Gonzalez. Would it be okay if we talk tomorrow?"

She sniffed. "Well, he could have just told me that."

"I apologize, ma'am," Jack said solemnly.

Mrs. Gonzalez accepted the apology with a queenly nod, backed out of the door, and tottered off.

I turned around and realized I was standing so close to Jack that I could smell him: the tantalizing scent of green forest with a hint of something sharp and spicy and very, very masculine.

"Are you *smelling* me?" He sounded amused. "I thought that was more a cat thing than a human thing."

I closed my eyes and prayed for the patron saint of pawnshops and stupid people to open a hole in the floor and swallow me. Unfortunately, nothing happened, which just reminded me that I hadn't been to church in nearly a month. Needed to add that to the list. It was getting to be a long freaking list.

"No. Allergies," I mumbled. "Sniffles."

"If you're allergic to cats, we might have a problem with this conversation," he drawled, clearly getting more than a little entertainment out of my humiliation.

Jerk.

"Can we just get down to business?" I retreated to my safe spot behind the counter. "We need to see Jeremiah's lawyer, Mr. Chen, and figure out—"

"I don't want to figure out anything, and I don't like lawyers. I told you, I don't want the pawnshop, not even for the chance to work with a gorgeous redhead with long legs and big blue eyes." He looked positively predatory when he said it, and I suddenly knew just how a field mouse felt when it saw the shadow of a hawk.

"I'm not a mouse," I said firmly. "You can keep your false flattery to yourself. We need to be legal about whatever it is you want to do. If you don't want half the shop, we need to work out a payment plan, and—"

"You can give me Fluffy for my share," he said, cutting me off again, and smiling a slow, dangerous smile that would have made my Aunt Ruby slap his face or shoot him if she'd seen him aim it at me.

I, proud of my restraint, did neither of those things. I also didn't leap over the counter and jump on him, which was pretty impressive, considering how long it had been since I'd had sex. Instead, I took a deep breath and tried to think of how to convince a thick-skulled tiger that we had to go talk to the lawyer.

A loud thumping noise at the back door interrupted my train of thought, and I jumped about a foot in the air. The roar of someone flooring a truck engine followed. Jack vaulted over the counter in a single leap, not even using his hands, and started to open the door before I could protest.

"Don't open it. It might be—" I was afraid to even say it. It couldn't be.

"Son of a bitch," Jack growled. "Tess, someone just dumped a dead body at your back door."

"Not again," I moaned.

He whirled around. "Not *again*? What the hell does that mean?"

My knees gave out, and I collapsed back against the counter. "That's how I found Jeremiah."

GET DEAD EYE FREE HERE!

ABOUT THE AUTHOR

Text ALYSSADAY to 66866 to sign up for my newsletter and get *free books,* release day news, behind-the-scenes scoop, win prizes, find out where Alyssa will be making personal appearances, and more!

Q: "What is the reading order of your books?"

A: Here you go: --> ALYSSA DAY BOOK ORDER

Alyssa Day is the New York Times and USA Today bestselling author of more than forty novels filled with kissing, laughter, mystery and magic. Alyssa's paranormal series include the Poseidon's Warriors and Cardinal Witches paranormal romances and the Tiger's Eye Mysteries paranormal mysteries. In an Alyssa Day book, the good guys (and gals!) always win and happily ever after always prevails!

Alyssa's many awards include Romance Writers of America's prestigious RITA award for outstanding romance and the coveted RT Reviewer's Choice Award for Best Paranormal Romance novel of 2012. She's a recovering trial lawyer who loves life outside of a courtroom. Her books have been translated into a zillion languages, but she's still holding out for Klingon.

You can hang out with her on Facebook (www.facebook.com/AuthorAlyssaDay), Instagram (@authoralyssaday), where she posts way too many pictures of her pug puppy and her future pug ranch, and her blog, where she talks openly about her crazy family, her rescue pups, her struggles with depression and more. (www.alyssaday.com/blog).

BOOKS BY ALYSSA

THE TIGER'S EYE MYSTERY SERIES:

Dead Eye

Private Eye

Travelling Eye *(a short story)*

Evil Eye

Eye of Danger

Eye of the Storm

Eye of the Tiger

POSEIDON'S WARRIORS SERIES:

Halloween in Atlantis

Christmas in Atlantis

January in Atlantis

February in Atlantis

March in Atlantis

April in Atlantis

May in Atlantis

June in Atlantis

July in Atlantis

August in Atlantis

September in Atlantis

October in Atlantis

November in Atlantis

December in Atlantis

THE CARDINAL WITCHES SERIES:

Alejandro's Sorceress *(a novella)*

William's Witch *(a short story)*

Damon's Enchantress *(a novella)*

Jake's Djinn

The Continuing Adventures of the Cardinal Witches

THE WARRIORS OF POSEIDON SERIES:

Atlantis Rising

Wild Hearts in Atlantis *(a novella; originally in the WILD THING anthology)*

Atlantis Awakening

Shifter's Lady *(a novella; originally in the SHIFTER anthology)*

Atlantis Unleashed

Atlantis Unmasked

Atlantis Redeemed

Atlantis Betrayed

Vampire in Atlantis

Heart of Atlantis

Alejandro's Sorceress *(a related novella; begins the Cardinal Witches spinoff series)*

SHORT STORY COLLECTIONS

Random

Second Chances

NONFICTION

Email to the Front

Author contact info:

Website

Email: alyssa@alyssaday.com

Facebook

Instagram

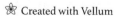 Created with Vellum